A Revenge Story

ANUSHKA ARVIND

PARTRIDGE
A Penguin Random House Company

To order additional copies of this book, contact
Partridge India
000 800 10062 62
orders.india@partridgepublishing.com

www.partridgepublishing.com/india

CONTENTS

Dedications

To my best friends (Pentagular).

Acknowledgements

I would like to thank my parents from the bottom of my heart who supported, helped and encouraged me throughout the writing of this book.

To the friends who always helped me get fresh ideas. Just when I write a page or two every now and then, they would immediately read it and give me feedback saying "Good twist!" or "Okay…" or even "Eww!"

Also to those who sneer at me and pass snide comments whenever they catch me scribbling stuff. It helped me a lot to do better.

PROLOGUE

I don't understand...why should I be the one to be in jail?! I hate being in jail...especially when I don't have anyone to bail me out. But it really sucks if you do have someone to bail you out but you don't know if they will come or let you rot in here! It was late at night and so the desperation of getting out was hurting me!

Well, why was I in jail?! How did I end up in the Police station? It isn't a big story, just a short one. My friends were out and they asked me to pick them up. I got to a main road and stopped nearby waiting for them. But they didn't come yet and I got worried. So I got down and went into an alley. They were coming and they were very tipsy. So I helped them into the car and they sat in the back seat while I drove. On the way, they got way too tipsy and were bothering me a lot but I somehow dropped them home. Like I said, it was late and I wanted to get home as soon as possible. But I was going a little too fast and the police stopped me. They just expected me to be drunk and they arrested me!

I'm complaining like a girl but I am one! I'm Sonia and I'm 20 years old.

It was a few hours but at 2:45am, I was bailed out... it was my dad's younger brother, Sameer. Damn, his big furious look.

At home, where I live with him, his son Arun and my aunt Naina, he started his lectures. I wasn't going to justify myself because he wouldn't believe me.

"Where the hell did you go and how did you end up in the Police station?!" he started, in fury.

"I will not tell you!" I said.

"Well, I hope you've understood by now that your so called friends are not the kind of people you should hang around with!" he said.

"Whatever!" I said.

"Don't test my temper! I'm not going to get angry now!" he warned.

"Then don't!" I said.

"Look, your parents are dead and they left you to deal with me! I'm letting you have a house, a bed, food and also I let you fix up your dad's bike for use too!" he explained.

"What's your point?" I asked.

"My point is that you should try to show some respect or else the next time you'll be in jail...I won't bail you! Got that?!" he threatened again.

"Yes..." I replied, slowly.

"Naina and Arun are going to come tomorrow morning! So just change and eat!" he said.

"Okay..." I said and went to my room.

My parents died in an accident. They were officers of the CBI. And they were killed in a bomb blast. They were in a building that was under construction and when the bomb blast occurred then the ceiling collapsed onto them while they were searching for the bomb with their friends. After their death, my sister left with my grandparents to Raipur and was there ever since. She's 16 years old. I stay with Sameer and his family in Bangalore.

Chapter 1
Plan B

The next day, in the morning, I left the house on my bike to go see my friends. They were fine. One of them had a serious hangover and another was literally puking in the toilet. They really didn't care if I was in jail or not. They took me for granted. I left from their homes on the way back when I passed the Police station that I was in...I shouldn't have done that! Two black cars came behind me and I had to stop! But I shouldn't have...because they weren't the police! This was bad! It was some other car...and there were men, with guns! They just grabbed me, shoved me in the backseat of a car and while we were driving away rapidly, I turned to see my bike! Blasted into pieces! Damn, my bike!

They held me down tightly! I couldn't move! I kept on struggling...but only for a few minutes because I knew that in a five-seat car with two guys in the front and back, fighting was not going to be a good idea!

By the way, these guys were professionals and they aren't so dumb because I was blindfolded by them. Hell, if I struggled more than they would make me inhale chloroform!

"No!" I yelled, while being in pain.

I was tied to a chair while sitting. I still had my blindfold on.

"Look! You don't know me! But I know you! Only too well! So you had better tell me what I want to know!" said a voice in front of me.

It sounded American. He took out my blindfold and threw it. I saw my surroundings. It was a window less room and there were a bunch of men encircled around me with two men in front of me with two huge guns. They all were in suits.

"Look! I've already told you! I don't know anything else!" I said.

"Neerav didn't tell you anything?! What type of daughter are you?!" he asked.

"How do you know my parents?!" I asked.

"All right, we're done here!" he said and opened a door then left.

The next thing...I woke up on the road with blood on my arm in pain! My arm had a bullet in it! I reached for my phone but it wasn't there! Damn, I left it at home! But fortunately I had a few coins in my pocket. So I found a nearby PCO and I called up Sameer.

He came within 10 minutes with Arun and stopped at the side of the road. I was sitting at a plastic chair near the PCO waiting and they found me. They picked me up and I sat with Arun at the back. When I explained what had happened he as usual didn't believe me, but when he saw my arm he did.

"Sonu di, where is your bike?!" Arun asked.

"It's blasted...ah!" I replied with difficulty.

"She's in pain! Let's get her home first!" Sameer said.

Since Sameer and Naina were Intelligence agents, they preferred to treat their own bullets. Also, they have to keep their cover so no hospitals. I realized my timing. I kind of deduced it. At 8:00, after leaving my friend's house, I was snatched by the men in suits. I was never a breakfast eater so every day at 11:00, I get hungry. But when I was thrown back on the road, it must've been a few 30 minutes after 11:00 because I had my stomach growling for quite some time.

At home, it was 12:07 and Sameer sat in front of me brooding while Naina took out my bullet then put a bandage on my wound. When the bullet was taken out, I bit my lip. Arun was getting me something to eat and I explained everything that happened to me in detail. After telling everything,

"His accent...what was it?" he asked.

"He looked American! I mean, he certainly talked that way too!" I replied.

"Were they dressed up?" he asked.

"Black suits and ties with white shirts. Why?" I asked.

He was wide eyed.

"Naina, we have to go to Plan B!" suddenly Sameer said.

"Plan B? What is Plan B?!" I asked.

I got puzzled and very much bewildered.

"Your father wanted us to wait! Arun, pack your bags! Naina, you too!" he ordered.

"Where are you going?! I'm coming too, right?" I asked.

At that question, he fell silent.

"What the-am I going to be alone?! Explain!" I demanded.

"You know why I trained you?! It's because your parents were murdered and they knew it! Look, they were not from the CBI, okay?! They were part of the NIA and IB! The ceiling did collapse but that bomb was put there by their co-workers! But you have to kill those people, they put a hit list for you!" he explained.

I was shocked. I had no idea about this! I thought that I was being trained for self defence! I was also kind of interested in it too! But no way!

"Hit list?!" I asked.

"Are you ready for your own mission?" he asked.

"Do I have a choice?"

"Look, it's all written in a letter! You just have to find it and kill them!"

"I can't kill! Don't be ridiculous!"

"You have to! You can't escape this! If you don't then they will kill you!"

"I have to be an assassin?!"

"I'm sorry but yes! You are ready now!"

I was in thought, and I didn't know what to do! Is he really kidding me?! I can't just go shoot somebody! I can but I never did! I mean, what is this happening to me?!

"Are you ready?" he asked.

I still didn't say anything because I was deep in thought. But then, after brooding for a minute or two, I finally said "Yeah, I'll do it."

"All right, it's simple to understand! Look for the hit list" – he hands me a piece of paper – "and this is the address of a guy your age who knows where it is! His parents and yours worked together! They got killed too! He also needs to do this with you!" Sameer explained.

"There's something bad, isn't there?" I said.

"There are many bad things which you have to face-"

"Just-tell me!"

"He's Rohan!"

"What?! That Rohan?! My-"

"You had a...something for him! He was in your batch of class 9 and 10!"

"No way, this can't work!"

"He's not trained as you are! In fact, he isn't at all! And the people on that hit list are very dangerous! In fact, you shouldn't have a permanent place to live! For now, you can stay here but then you'll have to clean out everything as soon as you get him and the hit list! Okay?"

"But, then where and how do I go?!"

"You can use my bike!"

"What about you? Where will you all be?"

"Cape Town. We'll be safe in South Africa. Do you know my new number?"

"Yes..."

"Good!"

"But Sameer...how..."

"I'm sure! I know you can do it! Okay?"

"Okay..."

"Now go to bed. Tomorrow morning, see us off! All right?"

"Okay..." I said then sniffled a bit and shed a tear or two.

"Good night, Sonia!" he said and left.

I went to bed, but with great difficulty.

Sameer says that I should be tough. Once, I thought that whatever target I was told to kill, it was dead anyway but then he told that they were very much healthy and alive when I had killed them. He's stiff, strict too. He never comforted me in anything and he wasn't going to in this. So he just "Good night, Sonia!" and left without giving any sign of care, caution or fear.

The next morning, I went to see off all of them. Arun came and gave me a hug first. I hugged back tightly.

"Promise me that you won't get hurt!" he said.

"Promise! You also promise me that you will stay safe! Will you?" I asked.

"I promise! Bye Sonu di!" he said.

He gave another big hug then went and sat in the taxi. Naina came next.

"Be ready from this point forth! You could get killed! But you must do this because we all are marked for death here!" she said.

"I know, I won't let you down!" I said.

"I'll miss you very much, Sonu!" she said.

"I'll miss you too!" I said.

"One more thing! Lighten up on Rohan! I know your history with him try to be honest with each other and work together! I hope you find his house! Bye!" she said, gave me a hug then got into the taxi.

"I hope you find uh, his house!" said Sameer.

"I'll need a team of others! I and Rohan aren't enough!" I said.

"After finding it, go on the highway to-" as he started to explain but I interrupted.

"Mysore? Will they still be there?" I asked.

"They will be waiting for you! Bye!" he said and started to walk towards the taxi.

"So your still mad at that jail incident?! I might never be able to see you again! You will never be able to see me again!" I said with a few tears coming out.

"Another thing! No delaying anything and train Rohan!" he said while still walking to the taxi.

"Unbelievable!" I said, pissed off!

He almost reached the taxi when he stopped at that. For a moment he stood there. Then he turned around abruptly and came to me. He immediately gave me a tight hug.

"I'm not mad! It wasn't your fault!" he said.

He pulled away, gave a kiss on my forehead then left. Wow, he really did care! After they left, I went inside and cried for 10 minutes. Then I made some calls and reservations. Then I immediately grabbed a bag pack, put a few things in it like clothes, my tablet, my phone, the address and my gun. Then I locked the house and left.

Chapter 2
The search

I reached the Yeshwantpur train station at 10:27am when my train was leaving from platform 3. I got in an AC 3 tier reservation and my train left in 20 minutes. The name of the train was the "Bangalore-Mumbai express".

Yes...Rohan moved from Bangalore to Mumbai so I haven't seen him in five years. He left after class 10. Anyway, I reached Mumbai overnight. At 7:30am the train pulled up at platform 5. I got down with my bag pack then I started walking out of the station. I booked my stay for two days a hotel and reached there with an auto rickshaw. I paid the driver, took my stuff and went inside. After confirming my booking, I went to my room then unpacked a set of clothes and I went for a quick shower.

After a quick shower, I took out a map of the city and the piece of paper which Sameer had given to me. I circled the areas on where he lives, where he might be and I finally found where he was held. Actually, I enquired in a friend's place and was informed that Rohan was snatched and was missing since two days! So I took out my tablet and searched that as well. It was 1:00pm and I put on a pair of jeans, a t-shirt and my leather jacket then I set off towards the address. I took another auto-rickshaw and stopped in front of a small lane. A tiny street. I walked in on the rest of the way and found an old apartment building of three floors.

The first floor had clothes hung; the second floor had nothing, only cobwebs and dust. So that meant that in the first or third floor he had to be there. But the first floor had ladies staying because I noticed only sarees on their clotheslines. The second floor had no signs of living because I went up and saw that every single flat door was locked. Locked and bolted. I went to a door on the first floor and knocked. A girl, who was at least 30, opened it. This conversation was in Marathi but I translated it.

"You looking for something?" she asked.

"I'm looking for a guy...this flat!" I said, giving the paper.

"Third floor...number 307." She said.

"Thanks!" I said.

"Please be careful! In that flat there are three guys with knives but when I saw them, they were drunk with one boy, age like yours maybe, black hair, styled, your height...they were calling out Rohan, Rohan and I haven't seen him come out after that night! So-"she started.

"I am capable of taking care of them! But why are you all staying here when you know that they have guns?" I asked.

"I can't do anything! My job is nearby and my family is having money problems so I don't have a lot of options!" she replied and I turned to go but turned around.

"Here!" – I gave her a card – "Go there as soon as possible! And yeah! I have intent to kill them. So if police come...then I wasn't here! Okay?" I said and left up the staircase while loading my gun.

I stopped at the door with "307" and put my gun at the back and tucked it in my jeans. I didn't knock...but I cracked my hands then kicked the door which busted open! I went inside and on my right was a wall in which a small TV was there. In front of the TV was an old couch on which three fatties with their dark complexion and a beer in their hands were sitting. I just casually leaned on the wall. In Marathi,

"Hey!" I said, very coolly.

"Hey...where did you come from?" asked the guy in the middle.

"What are you watching?" I asked, again very coolly.

"I asked" – while he gets up with the other two getting up after him – "where did you come from?" he asked again.

Three...two...one! It was lightening fast and I had already shot three bullets on each of them.

"Whatever!" I murmured.

Someone had heard the gunshots and in the room on my left, which was just bolted, someone was thumping on the door! I quickly unbolted the door and it opened...I found the guy which fit the description of what that lady gave. Rohan was tied with tape and his mouth was gagged. His eyes gazed at me, wide open and shocked. I rushed towards him, knelt down and took out the tape from his hands and legs and he spit out paper gagged in him.

"You're the last person whom I expected to show up!" he said.

"I feel like shooting you!" – While he yowled in pain when I took out the tape from his hands – "Get up! You owe me an explanation! Your place! Now!" I said.

"I'm still not able to believe that your here!" he said, while getting up.

He got up and immediately collapsed and I caught him in a reflex. He regained his balance and stood. He was surprised to see a gun in my hands.

"Who are you now?" he asked.

"Long story..." – he tried to grab it when I grabbed his hand and twisted it – "This is not school don't take my stuff! Let's go!" I said.

"Leave my arm first! Or you like to hold it!" he said, and I immediately let go of it.

"Don't act so smart, Rohan!" I warned.

"Oh good! You remember my name!" – I glared – "Well, you owe me an explanation too! Come on! My place isn't far!" he said then we came out of the room.

As soon as we came out and saw the bodies of those three guys, he was shocked!

"Who killed them?" he asked.

"Let's go!" I said.

We came out of the lane and started walking along the main road. In another lane, we turned inside and found a house at the end of it. It was as big as mine and we saw a few people about to leave. It reminded me of Sameer. But then I saw a familiar face...Dimple! Rohan's sister!

"Sonia! Your here! And you got him back!" she cried out and gave me a big hug then I hugged back. She pulled away and hugged Rohan as well. Then she immediately hit him!

"If I get to know that you touch another bottle of beer then you see what I'm going to do!" she threatened.

"Fine, I won't!" he replied.

"Sameer went for Plan B and they already left!" I said.

"We're about to go too! Explain everything to Rohan! We will miss our flight!" she said.

"I'll miss you, Dimple!" I said.

"I'll miss you too! I'm sorry he isn't trained! Good bye, Rohan!" she replied then she hugged us again and whispered into my ear "Your sister is safe with Sameer! Bye!" and got into their taxi. They all left.

"You're going to explain, right?" he said, sniffling.

"Let's talk inside!" I said.

He opened the front door of his house and I went in. He shed a tear as he closed the door and wiped it. I sat down after he did.

"Should I start asking the questions or you?" I asked.

"You've changed!" he said. "Leather jacket...hair tied...having a gun? Did I mention that you look really hot?"

"We're diverting from the situation! So just listen!" I said, while fixing my gun.

I explained everything that Sameer said and I even told him about the list and why they had to leave. He was silently listening to me. After I finished,

"Well, I know about the hit list!" he said.

"You should've told me! I wasted my time explaining it!" I said.

He smiled...just a bit.

"What?" I asked.

"I haven't heard your voice in five years! So I was listening!" he said.

"I'm going to forget I ever heard that!" I said.

"Okay...what else?" he asked.

"Is there anything to eat?" I asked, suddenly.

"What?" he asked.

"I haven't eaten in a day!" I said.

"I'll get a few things and the hit list! You can order something or...whip up something!" he suggested.

"Okay..." I replied and went to the kitchen.

Well, it was 2:30pm and at 6:37pm, we both sat down and ate dal and roti which I had cooked.

"I'd almost forgotten your food!" he said.

"Well, this is weird!" I said.

"What's weird?" he asked.

"You've said that I've changed when I keep remembering you as the one who would never notice me! Why?" I asked.

"Oh, I had noticed you in school! I always tend to do so!" he said.

"So why did you leave?" I asked.

"My uncle got transferred! And I thought that after the incident of...whatever, I didn't want to show myself!" he said.

"Okay..." I replied.

The thing was that I had a crush on Rohan so I just told him after pulling him to a side. Then I left without him saying anything. It was at out class 10 farewell. I didn't regret it again until now because I'm feeling really awkward.

"So we need to vacuum out this place! I've booked a couple of tickets in AC three tier! We have to be on the run now!" I said.

"That means we have to leave?" he asked.

"Yeah! Tomorrow morning, we'll leave the cleaning up to my friends! After they are done, grab a few things and then we'll go!" I said.

"Where are we going?" he asked.

"We'll take a train to Bangalore! I have to take a few more things! Then we'll ride to Mysore on my bike! Okay?" I said.

"I think I forgot how to ride a bike!" he said.

"I didn't!" I said.

"Last question! What are we going to do in Mysore?" he asked.

"We'll meet a few friends there! You have to train!" I said.

"Oh! To be an agent?" he asked.

"Something like that!" I said.

Chapter 3
The letter and the hit list

At 10:00pm, I grabbed a pillow and left his room. I went to the drawing room, which had no couch, and put my pillow on the ground. Then I lied down with the pillow under my head. Rohan saw and he rushed downstairs with a box in his hands and pulled me up by grabbing my hand.

"What happened?" I asked.

"Don't sleep yet! We have to see the letter and the hit list!" he replied.

"There's a letter too?" I asked.

"Yeah!" he said.

"Did you read any of them yet?" I asked.

"No. I had to wait for the right time!" he said.

"Good thing you did!" I said.

"Why?" he asked.

I narrated the incident of my kidnapping and unknown interrogation when I knew nothing at the time.

"Oh, well, I'm sorry but I didn't get anything like that!" he said.

He took the box and rummaged through it. After all, he never checked it for a long time. He finally found the two papers. Here's the hit list:

1.   *Sajid Aroura – CEO of 'T' – 50 years.*
2.   *Sarita Aroura – Ex. CBI detective – 50 years.*
3.   *Arjit Aroura – CID Officer – 28 years.*
4.   *Vipul Chawla – RAW Officer – 47 years.*
5.   *Deepa Chawla – RAW Officer – 46 years.*
6.   *Avanti Singh – NIA Officer – 53 years.*
7.   *Tanya Sharma – Cyber-police – 27 years.*
8.   *Pradeep Desai – Cyber-police – 30 years.*
9.   *John Ryan – CIA Agent – 37 years.*
10. *Amy Ross – CIA Agent – 36 years.*

There was a description below too:

"1 and 2 are divorced. 3 is their only son. 4 and 5 are married and 7 is their widowed daughter. 7, 8, 9 and 10 are a team of hackers."

Here is the letter:

Sonia and Rohan,

Your family now must have explained what you need to do. We are relieved that you both have found it. Targets 1, 2, 4, 5 and 6 used to be our friends and colleagues. We kind of knew this would happen because we knew what all scams they would do, what all scandals they would be in. This was written on the night before our deaths. We knew that they were manipulating us. We couldn't do anything about it and we couldn't turn to anybody for help. We are sorry that you are going to ruin your life like this. Definitely there are dreams of yours you would like to fulfil. But they don't deserve to live. If they all are killed then numerous scams and scandals will fall out and get exposed by themselves. But the most important thing is...Target 11: Prashant Oberoi. The mastermind amongst all of this is him. If you don't go after them first then they will come after you and your family. A team will be ready for you at Mysore. Take the NH 212 to Mysore and you'll find a restaurant named "Sanjana's". Go there and you will find them. Train very well and succeed on your mission. Burn the letter but keep the hit list. Love you and take care of yourselves.

Maanav and Rashmi
Rekha and Neerav.

Later on, we started catching up.

"By the way, how do you keep a gun?" he asked.

"It's safe, just don't pull the trigger!" I said.

"Where did you even get one?" he asked.

"I trained for 8 years with my uncle!" I said.

"Sameer? Wow!" he said.

"Well, good that you haven't changed at all! Except for that beard! Good night!" I said.

"What's wrong with this?" he asked.

"Take a look in the mirror!" I said.

"Whatever! Good night!" he said and then we both slept there only.

The next morning, at 5:00am, I threw a pillow on Rohan and he finally woke up!

"Ow! Can't wake me up politely?!" he asked.

"Polite is not my style! Get up!" I said.

"Style?" he asked.

"Start packing a few things before the vacuum guys deal with it!" I said.

The vacuum guys are specific people who come with vacuums and clean out the entire house of dust, fingerprints, hair, etc., in only a few minutes and they don't listen so much. They just clean and go. Rohan immediately got up and rushed upstairs. I heard a lot of noises of stuffing, hitting and opening of doors and drawers. I quickly yelled out "They will be here in another hour! You have plenty of time!" and he stopped, then came down.

"You could've said that before!" he said.

"If I did, you would've slept!" I said.

At sharp 6:45am, the vacuum guys arrived in their suits and they quickly cleaned the entire house! Since the people, who we are dealing with, are professional every bit of evidence should be destroyed or cleaned up, as Sameer said. Hopefully, after this entire mess is finished, I shouldn't see Rohan again.

"You got it all?" I asked him.

"Yeah!" he said.

I grabbed the letter. He handed me a lighter. I took it and lit the letter on fire then threw it into the trash and it turned into ashes very quickly. The vacuum guys left at

7:00am and we left too. At 8:00am we arrived at the hotel I was staying in and we both were in the balcony, talking.

"So..." he started.

"So what?" I asked.

"I still didn't understand the plan!" he said.

"Look, it's 5:00pm and our train's going to leave at 8:00! Simple!" I said.

"Wait! Where are we going?" he asked.

"I have to collect a few things from home...then we'll leave for Mysore!" I replied.

"We're going to Bangalore?" he asked.

"Yeah, I still live there!" I said.

"How will we go to Mysore?" he asked.

"My-well, Sameer's bike is there!" I said.

It was a quarter to 8:00 and we had already reached the station at Platform 7. While waiting, I realised that something was definitely wrong.

"Did our train arrive yet?" I asked.

"It's on platform 8! Why are we on 7?" he asked.

I turned and stood in front of him and then came a bit closer, uncomfortably due to his beard. Ew!

"We're uh, being followed...you see those two men in grey chatting on my left?" I asked and he turned to see when I pull his face towards me.

"You're too obvious! Okay...on my right is a man in grey sitting on the nearest bench reading 'The Hindu'!" I said and he glanced in a second and looked back at me.

"Only these three?" he asked.

"Don't be fooled! They are body guards of target 11! So here's what we're going to do! So keep up!" I said and went closer to him, not eying his beard.

We pretended to hug and I whispered everything into his ear.

"Okay?" I asked, while pulling apart.

"Done!" he replied.

We waited for sometime then we started to go up to the bridge. We started waiting at Platform 9, just to see them catching up to us. To make sure that they were, we sped up a bit. Again, we stopped but on Platform 6 where I saw that a train arrived at its last stop so everyone hustled and bustled out of the train onto the platform and created a crowd between us and those guys. That time, our train arrived at our platform and we immediately broke into a run!

We quickly got onto the bridge to see the train slowly going and the guys dash after us! We came down the stairs to Platform 8 and kept on going till the end of the platform where the shade wasn't there! They hurried down quickly and the train was gaining its speed! They were gaining on us and we almost reached the end! Before getting to the end, Rohan grabbed my bag pack, then at the last compartment door I immediately hauled myself in then pulled Rohan with my bag pack inside! The three guys were left behind! We made it!

The guys were definitely from Z security! They were of our last target! Well built, excellent runners! And they were fighters each holding an AK 53! They were sent to kill us already!

While the train moved, we walked through a chain of compartments and finally reached ours. As soon as we were away from the station and the city, we walked towards our coach, stowed our belongings under the seats and sat down. There was nobody else near us so we both were on opposite sides, looking out of the window.

CHAPTER 4
I'M HOME!

"You get the craziest ideas out of everybody I met!" he said.

"Don't call it crazy! Call it common sense!" I said, while smirking a bit.

"You did have that before!" he said.

"What?" I said.

"I mean, you still have common sense! I lost mine a long time ago!" he said.

"You'll get it back later on!" I said.

"What do you mean? By the way, you will kill them, right? It's just that I'm not comfortable with killing!" he said.

"Okay..." I said.

"So did anything change at your house?" he asked.

"No, it's still the same. Just how you saw it last...time. Okay! I will go order food! I just need some space now!" I said then went to the door of the compartment and stood there looking out of it.

I was uncomfortable...embarrassed actually. When we were in class 10, we both were held back for extra classes so after the class I started to walk home when Rohan was acting all polite. He walked me home and I invited him in. I totally forgot that Naina was there and she teased both of us! I felt like crap and so did he!

Anyway, Rohan came out and stood next to me after an hour. I kept looking outside.

"How...uh...how long are you going to be like that?" he asked.

"I've ordered two chicken biryanis. Fine with you?" I asked.

"Yeah...it's fine!" he said.

"Okay..." I said.

We both went inside without a word and got back to our seats. At sharp 10:00pm we received our food. After we ate I fixed my bed and he did too. Then we turned off the lights, I put my tablet and phone to charge and we went to sleep.

It was again 5:00am and I woke up. I fixed my hair with a comb and tied a ponytail. Then I grabbed my brush and toothpaste and left for the wash basin. After brushing, I came back, packed my bag pack and sat down near the window. When it was quarter to 6,

"Ow! Did you just hit me?" he asked, after I did hit him with a pillow.

"Good! You're up! Get ready! We'll be reaching in half an hour!" I said.

He got, while rubbing his head. Next, he fixed his sheets then bent to grab his toothpaste and brush then he left to brush his teeth. When he came back, I was eating a packet of chips and he got pissed off, or bothered because he started to look at me when he sat down.

"What's with the looking?" I finally asked.

"Nothing..." he said and was still looking.

"You've been looking at me for five minutes. What did I say?" I asked.

"Nothing! You didn't say anything!" he said.

"Good..." I said, handing the packet of chips to him. "Could you eat the rest? I'm not that hungry!"

He took the packet of chips and was silently eating them. Our station arrived and we got down with our bags.

"Your house isn't far, right?" He asked.

"You forgot?" I asked.

"Yes, I did!" he said.

"Come on!" I said.

We both grabbed our backs and left from Platform 2 towards the auto-rickshaw stand. I put our bags into one then we got in and left. After an hour of riding in noise and traffic the auto stopped at the end of my lane. We got down, paid the driver and started walking towards my house with our bags. It was at the end of the lane and was on...Fire?! It was on fire! And it looked like the fire brigade already extinguished everything and left.

"Oh My God!" exclaimed Rohan.

"Shit! My stuff!" I exclaimed with my hands covering my head.

I was so angry! All of my stuff! Gone!

"Sonia! Let's go check it out!" said Rohan.

I got up.

"The...uh...the fire saved us some money! Let's see how much is burnt!" I said and we entered inside.

Every single object in the house was burned to bits...as if someone came inside, poured kerosene oil everywhere then lit it up! When Rohan left to the kitchen, I went upstairs to where my bedroom was and everything was in black ash. With a bit of strength, I busted open my closet to see that my clothes were intact. I guess the closet protected them. I rushed down, grabbed my bag pack then left upstairs to my room and filled it with more clothes. After that, I went downstairs to see everything when Rohan calls out "Sonia! Help!" I quickly race towards the kitchen. When I passed the kitchen window, I was pulled down by Rohan and I heard gun shots!

"Please tell me that they are the police!" he said, getting scared.

I grabbed his shoulders. That calmed him down a bit.

"Even if they were, we will still be in trouble!" I said and took out my gun and loaded it.

"You got a plan?" he asked.

I nodded and told him.

"You have your bag and mine?" I asked.

He nodded.

"On three, take cover! One...two...three!" I said.

We both immediately got up, while the people started shooting from outside, I started to shoot back and Rohan took cover behind me. We both slipped into the front of the house with our bags and spotted Sameer's bike. It was a black Yamaha. I found the keys and two helmets on it.

"You can drive a bike?!" he asked.

"Yeah, can you?" I asked.

"Yeah!" he said.

"I'm driving!" I said.

Suddenly five big guys broke in and entered the house. We quickly put on our helmets, I started the bike then Rohan got on and we sped away as soon as I revved it up. We kept on driving and driving and we went as far away from the house and the city as possible. Since my house was located deep inside the city it took one and a half hour to reach the outskirts then on the highway. We kept going having no worries but after two hours I got tired of driving so I stopped the bike, parked on the side of the road then I took out my bag pack. I opened the first zip then took out my tablet. Damn, low battery! I tried the same with my phone but still low battery! I got frustrated so I sat down with my face buried in my hands. He plopped down right next to me.

Chapter 5
To Mysore

"What's wrong?" he asked.

"Can't you see what situation we are in?!" I said, very frustratingly.

"I mean, why did you stop? What's wrong?" he asked.

"First, I'm tired! Second, we don't have a map and third, I don't know who will come after us next!" I said, angrily.

"You think I don't know?! I'm even more freaked out and right now you at least know what you're doing! I don't!" he said and was getting scared again.

I sat up straight.

"Stop screaming! Don't that you're in this problem alone!" I shouted.

"Even you are screaming as if nobody is there here!" he shouted back.

We both looked at each other in anger for a minute or two. Then we stopped and I got up. He did as well.

"Sorry." I said.

"Me too." He said.

"Okay..." I said.

"Okay...this is NH 212!" he said.

"Saw the sign! I've come this way before!" I said.

"In 5 kilometres, there is a hotel with a restaurant!" he said.

"This road has to lead to Mysore! At least a 150 kilometres more! What's the time?" I asked.

"It's almost 12:00!" he replied.

"Okay...we'll just go eat something and get the gas tank filled. You drive!" I said and gave him the keys.

We both got on the bike and left. After some time, we reached. The hotel was good. So we parked the bike, went to the reception to book a table at a restaurant, went there and sat at a table. After eating,

"Do you have some money on you?" I asked.

"Yeah! Why?" he asked

"I'm going to go and fill petrol in the bike! We should leave quickly!" I said and left.

I said that because nobody was there...I mean that nobody was to be seen outside the restaurant, inside except the waiters and nobody at the petrol bunk. That was weird... the hotel staff was there, but only a few. Also in the reception at 1:23pm, where I went after filling petrol in the bike, I saw the receptionist leaving with her purse. I stopped her.

"Excuse me but where is everybody?" I asked.

"There is a threat! Police are coming to raid this place! They are looking for a girl and boy of 20 so either stay or leave!" she said and started to go when I stopped her again.

"Where are you going? You are 30!" I said.

"I don't see that as your concern, ma'am! A few staff will be here! They will assist you and your boyfriend. How do you know my age?" she asked.

"I'm a keen observer! And you're in a hurry!" I replied.

"Well, detective! I have a sick father at Apollo Hospital in Mysore so bye! Good enough for you?" she asked and left without an answer.

I did see a box of chocolates in her hand so I can just make a check later. But first, there's still that problem with this hotel and I wasn't going to stay here much longer. I rushed to the restaurant but before going in, I check back and that's where I saw two police vans! They had just arrived!

I went in to see two people grabbing Rohan and holding him down on the table! I quickly punched one guy and kicked another! I kicked the first guy then pushed away the second one! We both ran out with our bags on. Rohan puts on his helmet and tosses my helmet and keys. I put on the helmet and as expected, the officers snuck in through the back. We rushed to the parking, got on the bike and made a quick getaway!

"You filled petrol?!" he asked from behind.

"Totally full! I shouldn't have left you alone!" I said.

"You punch very well! How are we targeted always?!" he asked.

"'I don't know!"

"Did you do something before saving me?"

"No!"

"What did you do?!"

"I don't know what you're talking about!"

"Yes, you do!"

"I shot your kidnappers! They are dead because of me!"

"You shot them?! How the-"

"They were bad people anyway! They were going to kill you!"

"Why the killing?! They are not the targets!"

"Those people don't deserve to live anyway! And it's not like I will handle this predicament! I'm going to be an assassin and you will too!" I said.

He was shocked at that last sentence.

"Stop the bike!" he yelled from behind.

"The police will gain on us! I will not!" I said.

"Stop the Damn bike right now!!" he screamed right in my ears that I suddenly applied the brakes!

He immediately got down with his bag and started walking away!

"What are you doing?!" – he continued walking – "Where do you think you're going?!" – he kept on walking – "Rohan!" I shouted and he stopped then turned around.

"Well, I'm not going with you! I can't!" he said.

"You think that you're safe without me?!" I asked.

"I know that I'm safe!" he said.

"No, you're not! Trust me, if I leave you here, then in 10 minutes you will be surrounded by NIA officers!" I said.

"NIA?! What else have you done?!" he asked.

"I haven't done anything! Our parents just know too much!" I said.

I put on my helmet and got onto the bike.

"Are you coming or not?!" I asked.

"Where are we going?" he asked.

"Apollo Hospital, Mysore!" I replied.

"Why?" he asked.

"Stop asking why for everything and come on!" I said.

He put on his helmet and got on. I started the bike and we rode away.

We reached Mysore in three and a half hours. After entering into the city, we drove for half an hour on the main roads and found Apollo Hospital. At the entrance was an old friend of mom and dad. Her name is Sanjana Pandey, also known as the receptionist. I hugged her and she hugged me back tightly. After pulling apart,

"I'm glad your fine! I was worried! You did know that there were surveillance cameras, right?" she said.

"Yes, I did. How is your dad?" I asked.

"He'll be discharged tomorrow, he got shot! And-wait! Who is he?" she asked.

"You don't recognize him?! This is Rohan! He's my..." I started.

"So called boyfriend? It's okay! I know, he's Maanav and Rashmi's son!" she said. "You've grown a lot!"

"Thanks!" he said.

"Well, I'll join you guys later! Just head over to Sanjana's and you'll find Ajay, Simran, Raj, Ankita, Dinesh and Roshan!" she said.

"What about Sonam?" I asked.

"She's waiting for you! You think I'll lie about your best friend?" she asked.

"No, I just-haven't talked to her and-"I started.

"Go! You remember where, right?" she said.

"Yeah! See you later!" I said.

Rohan and I got on the bike and left the hospital parking. I drove all the way and in a few minutes we reached Sanjana's. It wasn't bad. Outside was Sonam waiting for us. I parked the bike and Rohan got down.

Thoughts raced in my mind! Sonam and I were best friends, yes! But we fought at the farewell of class 10. It was because of her being clingy to Rohan and when I had to talk to him she was pulling him away. I lashed out at her and then I was able to talk to him. But we never talked after that incident.

Rohan whispered "Sonam looks different!"

"Go flirt with her! I certainly can't talk to her!" I said.

"Hey!"- He grabs my shoulders – "Come on! We're still friends! Go!" he said.

"Fine! But don't mess around with her!" I said and left him.

I went and stopped in front of Sonam, just two feet away from her. We both looked at each other and she immediately hugged me and I hugged her back.

"I'm going to kick you later because you didn't call me in five years!" she said.

"Sorry...but so did you!" I said.

"Point! Sorry from here too!" she said.

We went inside the restaurant and went upstairs to a hall and went into one room with very less windows. It was a gym and a place to sleep.

"Sonia! Seriously! Where were you?!" asked Roshan and gave me a hug.

"Sorry guys! How could I know when Sameer told me a few days ago?!" I said.

"So with you both here...we're ready!" said Ankita.

"Not quite!" I said.

"Why not?" asked Dinesh.

"Rohan's not trained!" I said.

CHAPTER 6
DECISION OF TRAINING

"What?!" everybody was pissed!

"Well, isn't that swell!" said Raj.

"Our plans are in the drain now!" said Ajay.

"Sonia, if he has no skills then it'll take years to train-" started Simran but she stopped when we heard multiple gunshots and we immediately saw Rohan putting the gun down. All hit near the middle by him.

"Or a few weeks!" said Ankita.

"Not bad, Rohan! Where did you learn that?" asked Sonam, trying to flirt.

"Nobody! I just saw Sonia do it and I tried!" he said.

I was stunned on hearing that. Everybody was pretty impressed and surprised at that.

"Well, if he can learn that just by copying you, let's give responsibility to Sonia to train him!" said Sanjana, coming from downstairs into the room.

"What?!" I said.

"Yes, brilliant idea, Sanjana! We will scour the country for the others on the hit list so this full place is for both of you! Alone! For a couple weeks!" said Dinesh.

"A couple weeks?!" we both said that.

"Don't worry, Dinesh and I will stay!" said Sanjana, reassuring me.

That did give me some relief.

"Maybe I should also stay...to keep an eye on things, you know! They just got here!" said Sonam.

"Oh really?!" said Simran.

"First, I know this place better than you! And next, just admit why you really want to stay!" I said.

"Nothing! I seriously don't think you know this place well!" she said.

"Oh really?!" I said.

"Okay, guys! Stop! Sonia, you remember my gun vault? Open it!" said Simran.

"Okay!" I said.

"Sonam still doesn't know! Show her!" said Simran.

Without a word, I went up to the dead corpses and opened a crack in the wall. Then I pushed it and it slid open which revealed buttons. There were five buttons, one is in blue, one in black, two are in green and one is in yellow. I pressed the blue button and a floorboard cracked open. I took it out and showed it.

"Here!" I said.

"Okay! I'll go with them!" said Sonam.

"Good!" I said.

Everybody left to pack and later on, in my room, I was unpacking when Sonam comes to my door.

"Come on! Dinner!" she said.

"I'm coming!" I said.

"By the way, I just thought that I had a shot on Rohan! Like I used to!" she said.

"Oh so you used to actually have a shot on him! Whatever!" I said.

"Sorry!" she said.

"Just keep to your limits!" I said.

"Fine! He's yours!" she said, raising her hands in defeat.

We both did not talk for a minute.

"You saw Roshan? He's cute!" I said.

"Too good for me?" she asked.

"No! In fact, you should spend some more time with him!" I said.

We left downstairs. Everyone was sitting and eating at a table of the restaurant.

"So, you know how to start, right?" asked Roshan.

"Don't worry about your friend!" said Sonam.

"Yeah, Sonia will torture him a lot!" said Ajay.

"Yeah, that's why I'm asking!" said Roshan.

"How will you start? Shooting or archery?" asked Dinesh.

"Maybe with shooting. He's good with targets already!" said Anita.

"Cut it out!" said Rohan, smiling.

"Yeah! Let Sonia do whatever!" said Sanjana.

"Archery!" I said.

After dinner, everyone goes to bed.

So do I but at 2:00am in the morning, someone threw a glass of water on me! I woke up and wiped my face. After

I wiped my eyes, it was Rohan sitting there, laughing! Pathetic!

"What the hell do you want?!" I asked, angrily.

"Sshh! Someone will hear!" he said.

"Why did you do it in the first place?!"

"Teach me shooting!"

"What?"

"Teach me shooting, not archery!"

"Are you telling me what to do?"

"No, I know how you'll react to that if I say yes!"

"So you are ordering me!"

"Not quite!"

"Well, you're learning archery then shooting! After that, you'll learn combat fighting unarmed from Sanjana!"

"Are you kidding me?!"

"Nope!"

"Damn!"

"Now can I go back to sleep?" I asked.

"I guess, but-"he started.

"Come on, it'll be fine! We all won't torture you! I promise! Go to bed! If you got any problems then tell me anytime!" I said.

"Okay...see you later!" he said and went back to his bed then lied down.

After he did, I flopped back down on my bed covering myself and sleeping again.

In the morning, at 7:00, everybody got up and got ready in half an hour. Then we saw them off through the back as they left with a few bikes. After an hour, I, Rohan, Dinesh and Sanjana ate breakfast in the restaurant.

"For this week, you will be exercising with me, Rohan! We are going to go for a jog to the gym and back!" said Dinesh.

"After that, I will teach you combat unarmed. Then Sonia will teach you archery and shooting!" said Sanjana.

"Eat up quick and start now! I and Sanjana will go pick up her dad. He's being discharged today!" I said.

"Okay!" Rohan said.

He and Dinesh left after a few minutes for a jog. We both toured the place a little. We reached the vault of Simran.

"Do you remember why this bullet is kept here?" she asked.

"Yeah, I do!" I said.

Everybody always told me the story of why we never used that bullet. It was during the time Sameer and Simran were training together. They both were always the competitive type of people but always Sameer would put Simran down. Always! One day, they both duelled and suddenly Simran won! And that was when she shot that bullet in his leg! But she took it out herself and treated it.

Later on, we went to the hospital in a Mahindra and I was driving. We reached and he was being brought out in a wheelchair.

"Sonia, Sanjana! Good to see you!" he said, while standing up.

His name is Avinash and he is 62 years old. Sameer is 47 and Naina is 46. They were friends with him in the NIA. So were our parents. He was part of RAW and he retired.

"Hey, dad! Let's get you home!" said Sanjana and helped him to the car.

"Sure! Let's go! Sonu, will you grab my stuff over there?" he asked.

"Yeah, I'll just get it!" I replied.

I got his stuff in a bag and put it in the car. We all got in and I drove us back to "Sanjana's".

Chapter 7
The basics

At 2:00am again, after a gap of two days, I was awakened by a splash of water on my face by Rohan! Again!

"Is this going to be a regular thing with you or what?!" I asked, very irritated and wiping off water from my face.

"I'm going to have a problem with Dinesh! He's torturing me!" he said.

"You will be fine!" I said.

"If I'm not?" he asked.

"You will be! Go back to bed because you have to get up early!" I said.

"Okay!" he said and threw a towel on my face then went back to bed.

I wiped my face properly, put the towel and flopped back down on my bed.

In the morning, I threw a pillow on him to wake him up.

"Ow! Is this going to be a regular thing with you or what?!" he groaned.

"Deal with it!" – I looked around – "And put on a shirt, will you?!" – ignoring his beard – "I hope you're ready for weights!" I said.

"Weights?! That wasn't-"he started.

"Dinesh! Once he does stuff, he'll do it then leave it!" I said and left.

I met Dinesh in the corridor.

"Is he ready?" he asked.

"Nope!" I said.

"I've got this! Help at the restaurant! See you later!" he said.

"Sure!" I said and left downstairs.

I helped out Avinash and Sanjana in the kitchen of their restaurant. While I washed the dishes, Avinash served out his last order before his shift then came next to me and helped finish cleaning the dishes.

"How did Sameer tell you?" he asked.

"Surprisingly, he gave me a hug and kiss on my forehead! So, I guess he really is afraid!" I said.

"We all are, but he's lightened up. I thought he wouldn't after Shona and your parents, of course!" he said.

"Yeah, I know!" I replied.

Shona was Sameer and Naina's daughter, Arun's older sister and my cousin. We both were very close and she was murdered a few months after my parents' death. We don't know by whom and why.

After washing the dishes, Dinesh and Rohan come inside the kitchen, sweating after their dose of exercise.

"Hey!" said Rohan.

"Actually ran that much?" I asked.

"He sure did!" said Dinesh.

"Oh really?" I said.

"Yeah!" he replied.

"Well, if your little chat is over then get out of my kitchen! Your sweat's all over it!" said Avinash.

"Yeah, take a shower!" said Sanjana.

"Go!" I said and they both left.

"You sure that Dinesh won't be too hard on him?" asked Avinash.

"Yeah, what's he trying to do? Make him develop abs in two nights?!" asked Sanjana.

"If he does this then he develops abs in a week! Then he will be able to pick up a bow and arrow!" I replied.

"Okay..." he said.

Later on, during dinner, while we were eating,

"So how long do I have to eat this stuff?" asked Rohan.

"It's called a salad!" I said, while taking a spoonful of it.

"Oh, as if I don't know!" he said.

"A week should be enough! Well, eat quickly, we do have to get up early tomorrow!" said Dinesh.

"Fine!" said Rohan.

They quickly ate and left. I went to bed a while later. Before I slept Rohan came and flopped down on the bed. His bed and mine are side by side. His back faced me.

"You awake?" I asked.

"No! Leave me alone!" he said.

"You really want that?" I asked.

"Well" – he turned and faced me – "Could you tell him not to torture me?!" he asked, a bit too loud.

"Ssh! Just go to bed! I can't do anything!" I said.

"Fine! But I'm only going to do this crap if you do it with me!" he said.

"And if I don't?" I asked.

"You will! You like me!" he said.

"I don't! Good night!" I said and he shut up.

We said no more and we both went to sleep.

In the morning, I woke up and saw Rohan's empty bed. Good! He woke up early! I get ready and go downstairs to the tables to fined Sanjana ready to open the restaurant.

"Hey!" I said.

"Morning! Dinesh and Rohan went for a jog so they should be back later!" she replied.

"Cool!" I said.

"Oh! Breakfast hour is going to start and dad needs your help in the kitchen!" she said.

"Yeah, sure! See you later!" I said.

I got to the kitchen and saw Avinash.

"Morning! So, here's the menu!" – he handed me a slip – "Write that outside!" he said.

"Sure!" I said.

I took the paper and went outside. I started writing and after I finished, Rohan and Dinesh came back.

"Hey!" said Rohan.

"Hey..." I replied.

"What's for breakfast?" asked Dinesh.

"Take a shower first! You both stink!" I replied and went inside.

During lunch,

"You're getting fit now!" said Avinash.

"Yeah! You'll be trained in no time!" said Dinesh.

"Don't worry! Then it will be my turn!" said Sanjana.

"I told you! It's not that bad!" I said.

"Oh! By the way, Roshan informed that their job is going to finish in another few days so let's keep going!" said Sanjana.

"Got it! Rohan, start combat training tomorrow!" I said.

"Okay..." he said.

In the middle of the night, I was half awake. I was waiting for Rohan to bust in. After a few minutes, someone creeped in with a glass of water and was peeping through the door.

"I'm not asleep! You can come in!" I said.

He came inside and shut the door.

"Hi." I said.

"Hey...not able to sleep?" he asked.

"Yeah, I'm not!" I said.

"Same here!" he said.

"Why?" I asked.

"I...I just, I" he stammered.

"You what?" I asked.

"I miss Dimple! Okay?" he said.

"Oh...well, if it helps then I miss Sameer!" I said.

"You do?" he asked.

"Yeah, I do!" I said.

"Okay, what happened to you in five years?!" he asked.

"That's nothing for you to know! Go to bed!" I said.

"Why not?" he asked.

"Just go!" I said and slipped under my covers.

He didn't say anything and we both went to sleep.

Chapter 8
An old friend

After a few days of training with Sanjana, in which Rohan was being even more tortured, one night he flopped down on my bed!

"Dude, get up! You are sweating on my bed!" I said.

"Sanjana is even worse than Dinesh!" he said.

"Is that so?" I said and pulled him off and pushed him on his bed.

"Oh come on! I'm tired!" he said. "How long am I going to have to do this?!"

"You'll get through it!" I said.

In the morning, Rohan was still asleep. I got up and got ready in a few minutes and threw a pillow, again! Oh, I do enjoy that!

"Ow!" he said.

"Good! We will learn archery today! Let's go!" I said and went but turned around. "Put a damn shirt on!" I said and left.

After a few minutes, he came downstairs in the courtyard behind the restaurant.

"Finally, we're getting somewhere!" he said as he saw me painting a target board.

"Oh yeah? We are not getting anywhere! You are getting somewhere in your training!" – I threw a bow and arrow at him after hitting the bull's eye – "And you have to first do that to finish archery!" I said.

We started by me showing him the stance of holding the bow and shooting the arrow.

"I'm not getting it! I can't do it!" he said, frustrated and threw his bow and arrow down.

"Pick it up! It's the fourth time you've done that! I have been enough patient!" I yelled.

"No! I can't do it!" he said.

"Pick it up!" I said.

"No!" he shouted.

"Pick up the damn bow and arrow! Or else..." I started.

"I can't do it! It's too hard!" he said, while picking it up because he got threatened.

"In that case, you can do this for the entire day! God, you're so immature!" I said and stormed away.

I passed Dinesh on the way.

"What happened?!" he asked when he stopped me.

"I'm out for a walk! I've had quite enough of Rohan!" I said.

"Why?! What is so wrong with him?!" he asked.

"His tantrums, his beard, his impatience, oh him!" I said and left.

I went out for a walk. It was 11:00am. I passed an alley and was walking with my hands in my leather jacket pocket when a hand was placed on my shoulder and made me stop. Without looking back, I grabbed the arm and lifted the entire person from behind then flopped him on the ground! I saw his face only when he was still on the ground. Shit!

"Ow! You've gotten stronger, Sonu!" he said, with a familiar tone.

It was my senior, and my best friend! He was in class 10 and I was in class 9. His name is...

"Virat!? How!?"

I was not expecting him! I picked him up and gave a friendly hug! He hugged back.

"Sonia! I knew it was you! It's been years!" he said.

I punched him.

"Ow! Your still tougher than me!" he said.

"I know! But you never called! You live here?!" I asked.

"Yeah, you want to see my place? I think that Sweetu will be happy when she sees you!" he said.

"Was that cat ever not?" I said.

We both walked for half an hour till another alley. At the end, there was an apartment complex of two floors. We both climbed the stairs and reached his door. He opened it and suddenly Sweetu came and purred! Yes, Sweetu is a cat! A big, brownish and fluffy one! Always loves me! We both went inside.

"Sit! I'll get water or coffee?" he asked.

"Coffee's good!" I said, while sitting down with Sweetu on my lap.

"So...how is Aanya? Arun? Sameer? Naina?" he asked.

"All are fine and safe in Cape town! How is Rahul?" I asked back, while patting Sweetu.

"He reached Cape town safely! He was always interested in Aanya!" he said, while bringing coffee in a tray.

He puts down the tray and sits down with a cup after taking it from the tray. I set down Sweetu on a chair and grabbed a cup.

"So how long were you here?" he asked.

"I don't know, a few days!" I said.

"Cool! So did you start work?"

"No! Actually, one guy's still left for training!"

"Who?"

"Rohan."

"Rohan isn't trained?"

"Not at all! He shoud be shooting arrows now!"

"Oh, well! You do have a deadline! Hope you know that!"

"I do! It's hectic! How come you're not with me in this?"

"I have had enough fighting!"

"Dude! You are 21 and you've just started! We could use all the help we could get!"

"Look! I've already refused Dinesh when they came to ask, all right?"

"Come on! The more you refuse, the more delayed we get!"

"I don't think so, Sonia!"

"Come on, Virat! Please?"

"No, I can't!"

"Why not?"

"I can't forget the look on Rahul's face! I dropped him at the airport and he said 'Come quick!' with a worried look!"

"So?" I asked.

"I don't want to get killed! I'm the only one there for him! And I've been in a lot of trouble so that's a lot of pressure I will get if I join you!" he said.

What he meant was that he and Rahul were each other's life guards. They only have each other. They had to jail their own parents because when they were very young, their parents would beat them like hell! Rahul once got injured because of them! Since then, they were brought up by their grandfather. Rahul is 16 just like Aanya but she is tougher than he is, as far as I know. But she never sought to meet me. We never bonded in our one time we met. She never knew me, actually.

"I know your problem! But Rahul is safe! And you are very capable of living!" I said.

"I don't think so! You have any idea on who we're dealing with? Prashant Oberoi is the most dangerous person you have ever heard of! And I will definitely die in his hands!" he shouted at me.

He got up and I put my cup on the tray. He picked up the tray and put it in the kitchen sink then came. I got up then went to him and gave him a hug. He hugged back tightly.

"Sorry, I yelled!" he said.

"I'm sorry, that we haven't spoken for years! I'm sorry that I wasn't there for you! But I...I'll protect you!" I said, while pulling away.

"I still don't think so!" he said.

"You're my best friend, Virat! You were there for me, at school, at home! I owe you a favour!" I said.

"Okay...I'll think about it!" he said.

"Good! I should go! Check up on Rohan!" I said.

"Yeah, sure!" he said.

I cuddled Sweetu one last time then I left. At 12:30pm, I went to the restaurant and Sanjana came out.

"Hey! You're late! Come on!" she said.

"Sorry!" I said.

We worked till 6:00pm. After my shift, I went to the courtyard to check on Rohan. Just when I arrived, Rohan had done a bull's eye!

"You got it?" I asked.

"I think so!" he said.

"You want to practice a few more times tomorrow? Just to be sure?" I asked.

He was taken aback at the sentences I just said because since I had a long day, I merely gave tired suggestions in a polite manner to him.

"Yeah!" he said.

"Good!" I said and left.

I didn't feel to talk to him any longer. So I just left from there and lied down for a while on my bed. At dinner, while we five were eating we hear a knock on the door.

"Who could be here at this time?" wondered Avinash.

He got up and opened the door. It was Virat! He listened to me! Yes!

"What are you doing here?" he asked.

"I uh, I....I changed my mind!" he said.

"So you're coming?" he asked.

"I'm in!" he replied.

Virat comes inside and Avinash closes the door. They both come in and sit down at the table. Virat comes and sits down next to me. Rohan was surprised at that.

"You want anything to eat?" asked Dinesh.

"No, I ate!" he replied.

"Good to know!" said Sanjana.

We all ate and talked. Then Virat left to get his things ready and I went to sleep.

CHAPTER 9
THE BLAST!

The next morning, I woke up at the sound of arrows hitting the target. I got up and looked outside my room window, which faced the courtyard, to see that Rohan continued his arrows practice. I quickly got ready and I went down with a jacket on me.

"Hey!" I said.

He stopped and turned behind to face me.

"Hey!" he said.

"Were you up all night?" I asked.

"Yeah, and I'm not planning on sleeping!" he replied.

"Good! Go shower! We have our breakfast shift today!" I said.

"Yeah, I forgot that!" he said and we left in opposite directions.

Later on, after an hour, Rohan arrives at the restaurant with his apron.

"Sorry! There was no water!" he said.

"Yeah, whatever! We'll just finish our shift till 12:00 then we'll check on Virat! Okay?" I said.

"Yeah, okay!" he said.

We both started to serve out orders for customers at different tables.

"Virat looks different, right?" Rohan said.

"By different, do you mean hot?" I asked.

"Yeah! Thanks for making me lift weights!" he said.

"You're jealous, aren't you?" I said.

"Yeah! Who wouldn't!" he said, grabbed his order and left to serve.

Don't tell me! He shouldn't like me now! God, hell no! Why now?! I don't want to like him now but I don't want him to be with anybody else too! Oh, I should just stop thinking about this because it's confusing!

It was 12:00pm and I finished my last serve. I took off my apron and folded it when Rohan comes with his folded apron. We put our aprons inside, put our jackets on and went outside. While walking,

"So I guess, at school..." he started.

"What at school?" I asked.

"When you were correcting the karate teacher, you weren't showing off!" he said.

"Yeah! You seriously found out now?" I asked.

"Maybe I found out before but I remember that now! Also I remember that you were crazy for Virat but I guess that was for me to see and get jealous!" he said.

"Yeah..." I said, not looking at him.

Ugh, his beard! Anyway, we reached Virat's flat at 12:30pm. At the door, when Virat opened it, again Sweetu came but this time she went and purred in front of Rohan. He knelt down and picked her up then started to pet her. We both went inside and started to help him vacuum out stuff till 5:30pm.

It was 6:00 and we three started walking to the restaurant with Sweetu. While walking back, a mangy street dog popped out of nowhere and stopped in front of us. I was carrying a box when even I stopped. The dog started to growl. I immediately gave the box to Virat to hold and grabbed Sweetu. Rohan grabbed a pipe.

"When I count to three, Rohan, you attack! Virat and I will try to go ahead and get help! Okay?" I said.

"Yeah!" said Rohan, preparing himself.

"Your good?" I asked.

"It's a dog, Sonu!" he said.

I was immediately taken aback. He called me Sonu! After such a long time! He was going to do it! I counted to three and we both sprinted while Rohan distracted that dog. We reached the restaurant running with Rohan behind us. Virat and Sweetu went inside while I waited outside for Rohan. He came and stopped in front of me with his hands on his knees, panting.

"You handled it?" I asked.

"I managed to make it run away but it did scratch me and" he said, while panting.

"Oh no!" – I lifted his hand – "Come on! I'll put first aid!" I said.

We both went inside and straightaway went upstairs. Rohan sat down on a chair while I looked for the first aid kit. I found it in a drawer and took it out. I then went and sat in front of him with cotton and his arm.

"So, ouch! It hurts!" he said.

"I know! A minute please!" I replied, while dressing his wound.

"Ah! It hurts! Please! It hurts! Sonu, please!" he yelled and I stopped.

"Stop acting so weak and stop calling me that!" I said and went back to dressing.

"Fine! By the way, everybody else must be back already!" he said.

"Yeah…" – I finished bandaging – "Done!" I said.

We both went downstairs to the restaurant which was closed early for their arrival and preparation. Everybody was already down sitting at a table.

"Sonia! Hi!" said Sonam.

"Hey! How was the trip?" I asked.

"It was good! All successful!" said Roshan.

"So our new member is Virat!" said Dinesh.

"Oh, you couldn't stay away now, could you?" said Ankita.

"Interesting!" said Raj.

"Avi, when should we leave from here?" asked Simran.

"Yeah, actually we have to go to Mumbai first! Here's our target!" said Ajay and put a paper on the table in which there was a name written. 'Avanti Singh'. Number 6 on the hit list.

She was the one who tried to kill my parents before the bomb blast plan. She stood in a building at a blind spot near the cameras and tried to shoot them at a point blank range with a sniper but they dodged it.

"Oh, she lives in Delhi, right?" asked Sanjana.

"Well, you know the saying! It's always best to get a person not at home!" said Roshan.

"Wah wah! Kya baat!" said Sonam.

Everybody looked at her.

"Is it just me or a lot of things happened between those two when they were gone?" whispered Rohan.

"Same here!" I whispered back.

Suddenly Ajay coughed to grab attention.

"We'll leave in a few days!" he said.

Later on, after dinner, Sonam and I were on my bed, sitting and talking.

"So what's going on with Roshan?" I asked.

"Nothing! Absolutely nothing!" she started.

"You are my best friend! You still can't hide anything even five years!" I said.

"Okay! Okay! I like him!" she said.

"Good! By the way, will you teach Rohan some shooting only for tomorrow?" I asked.

"Yeah, sure! Why?" she asked.

"I have to pay a visit to a place tomorrow! It's targeted for a blast!" I said.

"How do you know?" she asked.

"I have my sources!" I replied.

I wasn't about to tell anybody on how I do stuff. Not yet, though. First, I had to find another friend of mine! Priya is her name! She is the most amazing combat trained fighter I've met! Her shooting is always precise! Her parents are retired but she is still alone. She poses as a very threat to the targets that we have to kill! A very dangerous threat! Virat and Priya! Together at school! Way too good. But they both were separated with distance. Too bad! But I'm not going to let it go so easily.

Sonam left to go sleep. Avinash came and asked "Tomorrow, you'd better wake up early, okay? I don't want her killed or with the enemy!" he said.

"I know! I'll get to her!" I said.

He left and went to bed.

In the early morning, I left the place on my bike and went to a small marketplace outside the Maharaja's Palace gate. At a snacks shop, I finally spot her going inside the Maharaja's Palace after getting a ticket. I immediately left money at the counter, grabbed a ticket and went inside.

She noticed me following her. She didn't recognise me! I couldn't believe it! She suddenly started to run! I was shocked at Priya doing this! She was my best friend! Immediately I sped after her and was about to catch her when she takes a turn which led to the marketplace of the Palace and stopped. She slowly turned behind. I slowly took out my gun.

"You were always a fast runner, Priya!" I said.

"I am, actually! You should be carefull with your gun. You never miss your shot!" she said.

I put my gun down.

"But I've led you here! There are no cameras of security guards!" she said.

"It's safe, right? Nobody can see us here?" I asked, while putting my gun in my jacket.

"Yeah, why?" she asked.

I rushed up to her and immediately hugged her. She was taken aback. But she squeezed me back with a tighter hug.

"Where were you in five years?" I asked.

"It's a long story, Sonu! Now I'm being followed by some men in black and white suits. I think I'm in trouble! I saw you at the market outside but I saw a few of them so I rushed in here!" she said.

"Don't worry! We'll get out of here! You have your stuff?" I asked.

She nodded. I ushered her to follow me. She and I left the market place and we headed the way back to the entrance. We almost reached the Palace gates when we stopped at the sound of a blast behind us!

"What happened?!" she exclaimed.

"The police are here! We should go!" I said and we both left.

We exited through the crowd at the market place. In a few minutes, we both reached the parking. While I took out my bike, Priya blinked a few times at it.

"What? Never saw a bike?" I asked.

"When did you learn this?" she asked.

"Long before! You hadn't known!" I said.

"Okay!" she said.

"Now get on!" I said.

She got on the bike, held me tight and we rode away.

Chapter 10
An unexpected surprise...

We reached the restaurant by 10:30am, at least. I parked the bike while Priya stood in front of the door.

"Hey!" – I put my hand on her shoulder – "What happened, Priya?" I asked.

"Him..." she said, while pointing to Virat in the window.

"Oh..." I said.

Actually, Virat and Priya! They were awesome at school! As far as I knew, Priya loved Virat! But i don't think I can say the same for Virat! He always flirts with other girls, even when they were together! I told Priya about this then she cried and broke it off with him.

"You know what? I'll leave!" she said and was about to go when I stopped her.

"Avinash asked especially for you! You don't care about Virat! It's been five years anyway!" I said.

"Okay..." she said.

She took a deep breath and we both opened the door. We came inside and everybody had stopped what they were doing to see Priya. Virat had gotten up! He looked so astonished at the sight of her! Rohan was with him and they came to us. Everybody went back to their work when they understood the awkward situation. When they did,

"Hey!" said Virat to Priya.

"Hi..." replied Priya, in an uninterested manner.

Suddenly Virat hugs her! This was not expected by both of us!

"How was shooting with Sonam?" I asked.

"It was okay, but you'd better teach me later again! Please!" he said, bending over to my ear.

"Sure, Rohan!" I said, not that I have gotten used to his beard. Eww!

Immediately Priya pushed Virat away from her.

"It's been five years! And you expect a warm hello from me?! If you do remember, I broke up with you! And I haven't called you or met you till now because I'm over you! So don't expect any hugs from me!" she yelled, angrily.

"But-"he started.

Everybody was watching the scene!

"No! Don't you get it?! I don't care about you at all anymore! Avinash and Sonu asked for me so I'm here! That's it!" she said, very sternly.

"Come on, Priya! It's been five years! And you still have to be angry about-" he started again.

"Shut Up, Virat!!" she screamed!

He said no more after that and stood silent.

When she broke up with him, he trash talked to her face! She was so hurt! The bad part was that she couldn't even beat him up because we were in school! That was almost making her depressed for a month! I couldn't take it anymore, seeing her like that so Sameer gave us two tickets to Ooty. On the Pongal holidays, we were there for a while, trekking up the hills and improving our stamina. She felt a bit happy whenever we reached the top. When we did, we would just sit on a rock and watch the view for a while.

"You're the best, Sonu!" she said, thanking me when she got better.

Yet what happened now was making her feel bad again like before. But she was handling it pretty well.

"Okay...that cleared the air!" I said.

"Anyway, welcome back, Priya!" said Rohan.

"Thanks, Rohan!" she said, at the most normal tone ever.

"Let's go find Avinash, shall we?" I said.

"After you, Sonu!" she said.

We both left and went upstairs. When we had reached the last stair and entered the room, Priya put her bag down. Avinash was sitting near a window reading a book with his glasses on.

"I found her, just in time!" I said.

"Just in time..." – he chuckled – "Wow!" he said, angrily.

He immediately put his book and glasses on the table and switched on the TV then put on the local news. It showed the Maharaja's Palace market place, where we were talking! That was the blasted area! Damn, the media arrived so quickly!

"You were followed by them! Sonia! Did you know?! Did you know about the blast?" he asked, very angrily.

"I knew that we were being followed! But the blast was unexpected!" I replied.

Well, I wasn't about to tell him that I knew and I lied because I was having a touching moment with Priya.

"Well, they were targeting you both!" he said.

"I'm sorry! I should have been more careful!" I said.

At that time, everybody else came inside.

"Look, we're sorry! We didn't know that they would do this!" said Priya.

"It's fine! But everything isn't okay!" said Ajay.

"You two put all of us in a lot of trouble!" said Simran.

"And they will find out later! Our location!" said Sanjana.

"Also Rohan isn't fully trained!" said Roshan.

"Are you done worrying?!" asked Avinash, out loud.

Everyone fell silent.

"We have 20 hours to pack up and leave for Mumbai! I will go to Cape town!" he said.

"But dad!" said Sanjana.

She felt bad.

"I'm sorry, but you all knew that this day was going to come! The blast triggered our presence. Now the entire Defence will be behind us in a few days!" said Avinash, trying to make us understand.

"Okay..." she said.

"All right! Everybody, start packing! We don't have much time! Priya, pack up Sonia's bag! Virat, pack up Rohan's bag! Sanju, I'll handle yours!" said Dinesh and everybody left to pack.

I also left with Rohan to train.

Dinesh and Sanjana go a long way. They were junior agents who were under my parents. Right now, they are engaged and they want to finish this then get married.

"That's good punching! Harder!" I said.

He punched the bag harder! This went on for quite some time. After that, we started shooting practice.

"That's good, Rohan! But fix your stance!" I said, after he practiced a few bullets.

"Okay..." he said.

He was about to shoot again when I stopped him and grabbed his hands.

"Dude! Look at the target! And keep your hands firm!" I said, leaving his hands.

"Okay, but it's a bit hard looking there! It's really easy to look at you, though!" he said.

"Stop flirting!" I said. "Now-"

I stopped because he wasn't listening.

"Hey!" – I snapped my fingers in front of him – "Stop it! Hey!" – I again snapped my fingers and he blinked, startled – "Stop that!" I said.

"Fine!" he said.

He was about to take aim again when Sonam called out to us saying "Lunchtime! Come quick!" and left.

"It's okay, let's take a break! Come on!" I said.

"Yeah!" he replied.

I was about to leave when Rohan calls out.

"Wait up for once! I'm coming!" he said.

I stopped.

"Seriously! What's your problem?!" he asked.

"Nothing!" I said.

"Really? Then why do you leave without waiting for me?!" he asked.

"I already told you that I don't like you!" I said.

I turned to go when he grabbed my hand and pulled a bit when I yanked it off and turned around.

"You've gotten a bit stronger! Just a bit! And I swear, I don't like you!" I said, going forward.

"Then why did you say that you like me on the farewell?" he asked.

That just made me stop right there. Shit! He just had to ask about that! I, what do I do?! What-wait! At that time, I heard a few noises! Of fighting! And shouting!

"Hey! You there?" he asked.

"Did you hear that?!" I asked.

"Hear what?" he asked.

The noise became louder.

"Someone's fighting upstairs! Roughly! Come on! I've got a bad feeling!" I said.

We both quickly rushed upstairs. The sounds became more and louder. Finally, we saw that Priya and Virat were fighting! Damn! I saw the sight of Priya punching his face! That has got to hurt!

"Hey! Break it up!" I yelled.

I went in between them, pulling away Priya. Rohan dragged Virat away to another room

"What the hell happened?!" I asked.

"A fight!" she said, wiping the bit of blood off of her mouth.

"And why did this fight happen?!" I asked.

"He was trying to talk to me! I told him to get lost, but then he just grabbed me! He was like, come on, baby! Give me another chance! And I said that I have had enough with your crap! And that I'm out of here! He pulled me saying wait! I should just listen and I wasn't, I...I wasn't about to! I pushed him back and was about to leave when he started to insult me! I got angry and-"she explained.

I hugged her.

"It's okay! I'm sorry!" I said.

"I don't know how to handle this, Sonu! I was totally fine for five years without him and now! He's there! As if he won't leave again!" said Priya, while sniffling a bit.

I called Sonam and informed that we will go down for lunch later. We both went to the terrace and sat down. Sweetu was there and she went and sat on Priya's lap.

"Hi Sweetu, I missed you!" she said and patted her.

"Yeah she sure does too!" I said.

"Why did you drag me here?! I'm not understanding that you are doing so much for avenging your parents! Why, Sonia? Why?" she asked.

"I don't have a choice!" I said.

"No! Do not give me that answer!" she said.

"I'm doing it for them! I'm doing it for Rohan! And Shona! Most importantly, I'm doing it for myself! Are you satisfied?" I asked.

"Who killed Shona?" she asked, after a pause.

"I don't know which target! But I'll try to find out!" I said.

"Okay...fine! I will be with you!" she said.

"And I can't thank you enough!" I said.

"But Virat is definitely going to be a problem! She said.

"Yeah, let me see if I can get Rohan to talk to him! Tell him to stay away!" I said, reassuring her.

"Don't worry! Rohan will listen to you! He always does!" she said.

"By the way, did you see his beard?" I asked.

"Disgusting, I tell you! I don't know when he will get the common sense to cut it!" she said.

"I hope he does!" I said.

"Speaking of him, there he is! I will go and eat! And yes, no fighting!" she said.

"Good!" I said.

She left then Rohan came.

"Hey!" he said.

"Tell me what Virat said!" I said.

"Oh, nothing! He's like, faking! Saying crap like he made a mistake, and he still loves her! Whatever!" he said.

"Okay..." I said.

"What about Priya?" he asked.

I told him everything.

"You're doing all of this for me?!" he asked.

"Not only you! For me too!" I said.

"But I thought you didn't like me!" he said.

"That doesn't mean that I don't care!" I said.

"You like me!" he said.

"No, I don't!" I said.

"I'm asking again! Why did you say that on the farewell if you don't mean it now?!" he asked.

"A lot can happen in five years!" I said.

"Why did you?" he asked.

"I don't know! I just did!" I said.

"Some answer! You hadn't even heard my answer!" he said.

"And I don't want to!" I said and left.

CHAPTER 11
LEAVE FOR MUMBAI

Everyone was at a huge table eating. I went to Priya as she had saved me a seat. I quietly sat down next to her.

"Hey! You both talked for quite some time!" said Sonam.

"Whatever!" I replied.

We all finished eating in half an hour and got back to work.

"Aim! Carefully..." I said, while Rohan was trying to shoot.

He shot a few bullets. All hit the inner rings.

"Try the bull's eye!" I said.

"I can't do that!" he said.

"Do it! Come on, it's not that hard!" I said.

I fixed his stance and grip.

"Red dot... aim and shoot!" I said.

"No. It's not working!" he said.

"Try!" I said.

"Sonu, it's not working!" he said.

"Would you stop calling me that?!" I said.

"I won't! What are you going to do?" he asked.

I went in front of him and close to his face, ignoring the beard.

"You can continue for the entire-"I started.

"Please don't say day! Please, Sonu!" he begged.

"Okay..." I said and I started to walk towards the target.

"Okay?! What are you doing?" he asked.

I was fixing the target properly. I then stood in front of it without saying anything and with my hands behind my back.

"What?" he asked, getting all confused?

"Here!" – I pointed at the middle of my chest – "This area is the red dot! Shoot it!" I said.

"Are you crazy?! No!" he said.

"Yes, I am! So shoot!" I said.

"No! I can't do it!" he said.

"You like looking at me, right? Go ahead!" I said.

He looked at me for a while to see whether I was joking or not, then took his position. I braced myself and put my hands behind my back.

"I can't!" he said.

"Do it!" I said.

"I told you! I can't!" he said.

"Do it! It's so easy! Aim and shoot! Aim and shoot, Rohan! Come on! Do-"he shot! And immediately I bit my lip and fell back on the target and collapsed down.

"Shit!" Rohan immediately dived near me.

"You did it! Now you know the feeling of hitting someone!" I said.

"Are you crazy?!" he exclaimed.

"Relax!" – I grabbed his hand and he pulled me up – "It didn't hit me!" I said.

"Why?! Aren't you hurt?!" he asked.

I pulled the bullet off of my chest.

"First rule of defence! Wear a bulletproof chest!" I said and threw the bullet away.

He was astounded at that and was just looking at me.

"You are so crazy!" he said.

"Common sense!" I said.

"Okay! Common sense!" he said.

"Good! I guess, that's it!" I said.

"What do you mean by 'that's it'?" he asked.

"That's it! Training's over! I'm going to go pack!" I said and left.

"Yes! Yes! Yes!" he happily pranced at that.

He was happy. I left and reached my room but then pulled myself back. Sonam was packing! She was packing my bag! I kept still and pressed a button on my glasses, she was putting something in there. It looked like some packet...of white powder in it. One word popped in my mind: Drugs. Where did she get those? Why is she putting it in my bag? And she had me fooled for a while that she was still my friend. I just always had a doubt.

At that time, I had my glasses on. Sameer had installed a camera on it. And I had immediately pressed record. I came inside after she zipped up my bag.

"Hey!" I said.

She took a huge breath and turned around.

"Hey! Your bag's packed!" she said.

"Yeah, well, I'm tired!" I said and I lied down on my bed.

"Yeah! Me too! I had to pack two bags. Mine and Roshan's!" she replied.

Good actress, I have to admit. But not good enough for me. I will definitely keep an eye on her. At dinner,

"Okay, listen! For organising, transport and stay, Dinesh is in charge! And of course, all the planning and attacks go to Sonia! Also, for alarms to wake up everyone, Priya is there! Do be careful!" said Avinash.

"Yeah!" everybody replied.

"Why does Sonam still hate you?" Rohan immediately whispered after noticing her.

"What did she do?" I asked.

"Her expression wasn't good when Avinash put you, Dinesh and Priya in charge! Come on! It was bound to happen!" he said.

"I don't know either! Leave it! She doesn't know that I'll always have an eye on her!" I said.

"Yeah, you always will! You're great!" he said.

"So...you were happy today!" I said, diverting.

"Yes! Now it's done!" he said.

"Not so fast! We haven't even started our hunt yet!" I said.

"Please! Don't say it like that! I still have problems of killing!" he said.

"In that case, I will make sure you do!" I said.

In the early morning, while Avinash was packing inside, we all were deciding on the vehicles seating arrangements outside. We had three bikes and one black Mahindra.

"Okay, my bike is for me and Sanjana!" said Dinesh.

"Same here! My bike is for me and Ankita!" said Raj.

Raj and Ankita were Rohan's parents' junior agents. They have been married for a year. They were suggested to go to Cape town with Avinash but they refused.

"Sonia, who would you like?" asked Raj. "Or you'll let somebody else drive!"

"My bike, my rules!" I said.

I was going to say Rohan but then I saw Priya coming.

"Priya will ride with me, right?" I said, and turned to her.

"Yeah!" she said.

While everybody else decided, Rohan suddenly called me aside.

"Why Priya?" he asked.

"You should understand! Do you know how many people I have to support because they are emotional?!" I said.

"Yeah, but I-"he started.

"Oh! You like to ride behind me!" I said.

"Yeah, I do! Come on!" he said.

"We can't afford any mistakes in what we're doing here! So as much as I would love to patch them up, I won't! Okay?" I said.

"Fine!" he said.

After a few minutes, Avinash came. But before that, while I was talking to Rohan, I took out the drug packet and put it in Sonam's bag.

"She put that in your bag? What is it?" he asked.

"Ssh! She put this drug packet so I am putting it back!" I said.

We all gave our good byes to Avinash.

"You have to do this! Hope you stay alive!" he said to me.

"I will!" I said.

We all left. Avinash left with Sweetu to the airport. In a few minutes, there was a fork in the road. Avinash took the right way while we went left. We reached NH 57 in an hour. Later on, we reached Bangalore again but I didn't stop at home. After four hours, we then stopped for our breakfast at a small restaurant.

"You go a bit too fast, Sonu!" mentioned Priya.

"You like it? Or hate it?" I asked.

"Of course, I love it!" she said.

"Damn, where were you for five years?" I asked.

"Home, spending the last few days with Dad!" she replied, a bit gloomily.

"What do you mean in last few days? What happened?" I asked.

"For three years, I was training comfortably with my parents when my dad was admitted with cancer. Skin cancer. He died in his operation and..." she wouldn't say further.

"I'm sorry! I-"I started, apologetically.

"It's okay! You didn't know! Anyway, I sent mom to Cape town!" she said.

"Good!" I said.

We started again after finishing our breakfast. It took 16 hours to reach Mumbai. After another hour we reached our hide out. It was an old warehouse garage.

CHAPTER 12
FIRST TARGET!

We entered inside and parked. Then we unloaded our stuff and started unpacking in two old rooms. The girls were in one room and the guys were in another. In the girls' room, Sonam unzipped her bag and immediately zipped it back up again! Priya noticed that.

"Sonam?" she asked.

She was not opening her bag. She definitely saw the packet.

"Hey! What happened? Are you feeling uncomfortable or what?" I asked.

She again took a deep breath and slowly turned around.

"What happened? Sonia, did you do something?" asked Sanjana.

"I didn't do anything!" I replied.

"Oh really? Who" – she took out the drug packet from her bag – "put this in my bag then?!" she questioned me!

Wow! She still wasn't admitting, huh!

"Good show, Sonam! It's better if you tell now otherwise I won't hesitate to" – while taking out her gun – "use this!" Simran threatened.

She was serious, of course! Simran is the most rowdy person I have ever met! And she would not joke around! Recently, during Sonam's training, before I got to Mysore, Sanjana told me that Simran had shot Sonam on her thigh just because she didn't listen to her! Damn!

I showed the footage of Sonam putting the drug packet in my bag on my glasses. Everyone was wide-eyed. Sonam blabbered everything out of fright!

"Why?" asked Simran, sternly.

"Because it is always Sonia and Rohan! Always has, always will!" she yelled.

Damn, what a liar.

"Just so you know, it's supposed to be Sonia and Rohan! It's revenge for their parents! Yours are fine! Thank your horses for that! Why did you even join if you're so selfish always?!" scolded Ankita, after shutting the door.

"That reason is not the real deal isn't it?" said Priya.

"No, it's not!" Sonam said.

"Then what?" asked Simran.

"What you all are doing is wrong. And I don't want you all to do it then go to jail!" she said.

"Look who's talking!" said Sanjana.

"I did petty things, I regretted them later!" said Sonam, defending herself.

"Petty things, my ass!" said Priya.

Petty things? I don't think so! Sonam was a highly trained professional thief of National artefacts. She was a mercenary. Putting Indian artefacts for auction did give a great price in the market. But of course, she was right. She only stole whereas we are about to kill. That's a huge difference. But if we don't do it then they will kill us.

"Enough, guys!" I finally spoke up.

Everybody fell silent.

"We are friends, am I right? If you don't value anything then you can leave!" I said, with a pointed finger.

"No! And run away to Cape Town like the others?! Face it! You need me here!" she said.

"They didn't run away! It's not their fight so we sent them somewhere safe!" said Simran, clicking her gun.

Oh shit! Was she going to do it?! Wait!

"Simran! Come on! I know that you'll do it! And we know that she knows you'll it again but that is not the solution!" I said, softly.

She nodded and lowered her gun.

"So, are you going to stay? Or leave?" asked Priya.

"Stay..." said Sonam.

"Good!" I said.

"But let's just be clear! I'm watching you!" said Simran.

Immediately we all were interrupted with the knocking on our door. Simran opened it and we saw Rohan and Roshan.

"Yes, Roshan! Come to defend Sonam?!" asked Simran.

"No!" said Roshan.

"Dinesh called for dinner in five minutes!" said Rohan.

"Okay! Five minutes!" I replied and they left.

Simran shut the door.

"So are we done here?" I asked everybody in the room.

"Yes..." they replied.

"Good! Let's go!" I said.

Everybody came after I opened the door. We went to the garage main hall where Dinesh and the rest of the boys were sitting and waiting with take-out food.

"Good! Let's eat!" said Ajay, as he got up and pulled Simran over next to him.

Ajay and Simran go back a long way. They were married by arranged ways and they hated each other! So much! They once beat each other up! That's when they started getting doubts on each other's jobs. After they found out who they really are, they started getting acquainted. They are more than comfortable now.

He had heard all the cat fight going on! All of them did! So he quickly made Simran sit with him. I sat down next to Rohan. While eating, I tell him everything.

"Damn!" he said.

"I know..." I said.

"Thank goodness Simran was there!" he said.

"Yeah, she believed me!" I said.

"Don't worry! Everybody else will get to believe you too!" he said.

"Yeah, let's see! What about you?" I asked.

"What about me?" he asked.

"You'll believe me or not?" I asked.

"Seriously? This is no doubt! I like you and I will always believe you!" he said.

"Okay...awkward!" I replied.

We all continued to eat.

Early in the morning, we got up and started to plan in the main garage hall.

"Morning, everybody!" I said.

"Morning!" everybody replied.

I took out a map of the layout of the hotel which would have Avanti Singh seen there.

"Here's the entrance and the backside! Now the plan is kind of hard. But listen carefully!" I said.

Everybody listened to the plan carefully. While going to the hotel, Rohan asked me numerous doubts, some repeated. He was nervous.

Later on, after lunch at that hotel with my old friend Jai, one of my cousins, we were getting along with the staff as they were also a part of this too.

"How've you been, Sonu?" he asked.

"I would lie if I would say fine!" I replied.

"What would you say then?" he asked.

"In a dangerous situation!" I said, and noticed Rohan calling me. Jai also noticed that.

"So who's your boyfriend over there?" he asked.

"He's not my boyfriend! That's Rohan!" I said.

Jai grinned and left. Rohan came close to me and I moved back a bit.

"Everybody's ready in their places! Bluetooth's will get activated at 7:00! Sharp!" he said.

"Good! Everybody remembers the plan?" I asked.

"Yeah! Will you...uh, tell one thing?" he asked, coming closer.

I moved back again. I can't stand being close to that beard of his. I think he finally understood that because when I did that he immediately put his hand on his beard.

"Not, not now! Later! We've got work to do!" I said.

The target was coming as a proxy for her boss Prakash, of course. And it should be easier to shoot her that way, in the spotlight. It was evening, at 7:00 sharp our Bluetooth devices turned on. Guests started to arrive and they entered the ballroom. The ballroom was a huge hall with balconies just surrounding it. I quickly grabbed Rohan and pulled him into the kitchen. I had to get somebody to fix my tie on my waiter vest. I was to serve drinks on trays. I had no idea on how to fix one.

"What do you want?" he asked.

"Could you fix my tie?" I asked.

"What? Can't do it yourself?" he asked.

"Don't attract attention! Do it!" I said.

"Okay! Stand straight!" he said.

"Don't think anything different about this, got it?" I warned.

He fixed the tie. Then he lifted my collar and put the tie around it then tightened it. Then he fixed my collar. He was about to leave when I say,

"Hey, wait!" I said.

"Yeah?" he replied.

"How do I look?" I asked.

That's when everybody in the kitchen looked at us with Jai. Rohan was wide-eyed.

"You're asking me this?" he asked.

"I pulled you in, didn't I?" I said.

"You look good! Go!" he said.

"See you later! And Jai, you can stop smiling!" I said and left with a smirk.

Damn! Why did I just do that? Anyway, I entered the ballroom and stood next to Virat at the bar and collected a tray of drinks from him. I served them out and went back to the bar. While collecting more,

"So..." – while putting the tray down – "anything interesting with Priya? Or she'll still want to smack you like before?" I asked.

"I don't know! I think that she's controlling her anger in front of me!" he replied.

"Well, you acted like a jerk to her!" I said.

"But I've changed! I did!" he said.

"I know you did! Convince her that!" I said.

Just then we both saw the target arrive. Immediately after a minute,

"Sonia, we took care of her bodyguards! All clear!" said Dinesh, who was with Raj and Simran.

"Good!" I said.

"Sonu, we checked her car. There's cash and we collected it." Said Rohan, who was with Sanjana and Roshan.

I was waiting for the last call from Priya, Ajay, Sonam and Ankita. They were supposed to fill the gas tanks of the bikes. For five minutes I was waiting then finally Priya called.

"Bikes and car is ready! All clear here!" Priya called.

I grabbed an empty tray and started to collect glasses from the tables. I roamed around the ballroom till I got a good place to shoot from.

"Sonu, she just left the bar!" said Virat.

"I got it!" I said.

I saw her in the middle of the room. I wore my mini-gun on my finger and the silencer on it.

"All right, guys! I'm doing it now!" I said and I started to walk towards her.

She doesn't notice me passing by. As soon as I did, I swiftly twirl my fingers to her stomach and it shot out three bullets to her stomach. After that, she immediately collapsed. I quickened my pace and exited out the building. I looked back and saw Rohan coming behind me after shooting one bullet in her chest. I then switched off my Bluetooth. We all did. After an hour, everybody came back to the warehouse and started to pack. After packing, we assembled in the main garage hall.

"Tomorrow, we leave here at 5:00am sharp, okay?" said Dinesh.

"Yeah..." everybody replied.

"Good job, guys! Good night!" I said.

We woke up early. As we loaded our stuff,

"Can I...uh...ride with you?" asked Rohan.

"Yeah, sure! You had to ask that thing, right?" I asked.

"No! Leave it!" he said.

He left. Priya came to me.

"Hey, will you go in the car today?" I asked.

"All right!" she said.

"No problem, right?" I asked.

"I can handle him now!" she said.

"Okay!" I said.

We all left Mumbai at sharp 5:00 in the morning. In half an hour we were on a highway going to Nagpur as our next target Sajid Aroura is attending a convention at another hotel and will be there. If he's smart enough, he'll know that we're after him. As far as I know, or remember, he's a total fraud. He had close connections with my parents so he knew their entire schedule.

Chapter 13
Next aim, doubts

We stopped on the NH 3 near the town of Dhule at a dhaba for breakfast.

"Hey!" – Noticing Roshan deep in thought – "What's wrong?" I asked.

"It's okay! It's nothing!" he said.

"No, it's not okay! Tell me!" I said.

"Later, Sonia! Not here!" he said.

"Ride with me!" I said.

"Okay..." he replied.

Later on,

"Just till lunch!" I said because Rohan was getting annoyed about this.

"Oh, come on!" he said.

"Stop acting so bothered!" I said.

"I am bothered!" he replied.

"Well, stop it! Otherwise-"I started.

"Otherwise! It's always otherwise for you!" he said.

"Yeah, it is! So deal with it! Got that?!" I said, pointing at him.

"No!" – He grabbed my hand – "I don't! You're so hard to get!" he said.

"Shut up, Rohan!" I said, while pulling my hand back.

"You know, seriously? Ever since I got in this mess with you, I've been ordered around by you! I don't like it! I know how to do shitty jobs now!" he said.

"No, you don't! I've killed before, Rohan! More than you! I know! You don't! I order you around? Come on! Who would do that in high school?!" I asked.

"So what? You're just getting back at me?!" he asked.

"I'm just showing that this is my turf now! Not yours!" I said.

"Really?" he asked.

"Yeah, now stop yelling! I wouldn't get back at you!" I said.

He paused for a while.

"Hey! Dude, say something!" I said.

"Sorry..." he said, softly and left.

He passed Roshan and got in the car. Roshan came.

"All good?" he asked.

"Yeah! Let's go!" I said.

I got on and started the bike. He got on behind me. We all started to drive on NH 6.

"Actually, it's Sonam!" he started.

"So what's the problem with Sonam?" I asked.

"I'm supposed to hate her! But I don't know why I...I like her!" he said.

"Wow! I do not understand the problem here!" I said.

"I don't trust her. She is pretty determined on stopping what we are doing here! I mean, after that argument, I don't think I should say anything to her! But I want to! But I'm afraid too and it's confusing!" he said.

"Okay! I get it! But do you think she's with the enemy?" I asked.

"I don't believe that!" he said.

"Woah! Okay!" I said.

"So? What to do?" he asked.

"Okay...for now you wait! I still have doubts on her!" I said.

"I know, so do I!" he said.

"After this target, I can tell you what I think you should do!" I said.

"Good idea! Thanks!" he said.

"No problem!" I said.

"By the way, Rohan still likes you!" said Roshan.

"Please, not him! He changed anyway!" I said.

"Changed? He's exactly the same!" he said.

"Did you see his beard? Gross!" I said. "One of the main problems of him!"

"His beard is bad! But he still does!" he said.

"Still? Did he ever like me?" I asked.

"He did! He was just too cool! But even after our tenth, he kept on calling to ask about you!" he said.

"Wow! Interesting!" I said.

We stopped at 1:00 for lunch. He got down and then I parked.

"Well, thanks!" he said.

"No problem!" I said.

We left and caught up with the others in a restaurant. While eating,

"Can I still ride with you later?" asked Rohan.

"Yes..." I replied.

"By the way, any updates?" asked Priya.

"You tell me! You sound happy!" I replied.

"No, nothing! Actually, Sonam started to ask various questions to embarrass Virat! So I just enjoyed!" she explained.

"Oh! That's a good sign!" I said.

"Don't! I'm just satisfied!" she said.

"When are you going to forgive him? He changed!" I said.

"I already did that! But I'm over him! I don't have anything for him!" she said.

"But you both can be friends, right?" I said.

"Yes, we can!" she replied.

After lunch, we started again. This time, Rohan was riding behind me. At 5:00 in the evening, we reached Nagpur and went to an old apartment. It was of two floors and on the top floor, we had two flats. We went inside and unpacked our bags. Without hesitation, Sonam also normally unpacked her bag. I looked at Sonam then at me and winked. She did something. But I don't know what. Simran didn't shoot her. Then what? And I thought I handled it.

"Hey!" I said, while pulling her to a side in a room.

"What?" she asked.

"You did something! Sonam is totally afraid!" I said.

"I just threatened her!" she said.

"You don't have to do that, Simran! I can take care of myself and this team!" i said.

"But it's my duty!" she said.

"What do you mean?" I asked.

"I've been appointed as your guardian with Sameer!" she said.

"Guardian? Like parent? No-"she closed my mouth when I said that.

"Ssh! Not so loud! Yes, I am! And Ajay is Rohan's!" she said.

"Mom hired you?" I asked.

"Yeah! And I didn't stay around because Sameer didn't want me there!" she said.

"But you kept visiting!" I said.

"They didn't tell me to, I'm doing it for them! I did want to see you! But Sameer's restrictions were to be followed! You're like my kid! Okay?" she said.

"Thanks, Simran!" I said.

"Are you okay?" she asked.

I sniffled a little and looked up so that my tears would seep back into my eyes.

"Yeah, but don't stick!" I said and left.

I went outside. I saw everybody unpacking but I didn't spot Rohan anywhere.

"If you're looking for Rohan, he's on the terrace. He wanted to be alone! I don't know what happened to him after talking to Ajay!" said Virat.

"Yeah, thanks!" I said and sniffled a bit.

"Are you okay?" asked Priya, when she noticed.

"You two talk! I'll be right back!" I said and left upstairs.

I opened the door leading to the terrace and found him sitting in a corner, with tears rolling down his face.

"Rohan?" I called out as I went to him.

He immediately wiped his face.

"What?" he asked.

"Care to tell me everything?" I asked.

"I think you already know that Ajay is my guardian!" he said.

"And Simran's mine!" I said. "I can leave if you want me to!"

"It's your wish!" he said.

I kneeled down in front of him. He was just sitting with his knees up.

"Why don't you feel like crying?" he asked.

"I do have feelings but I can't cry!" I said.

"Why is it like that?" he asked.

"I don't know. Okay? Now get up! We have to go plan out our next move!" I said.

"Yeah..." he got up and I did.

He rubbed his eyes and left downstairs. When we reached, everyone was assembled and waiting for us. Rohan immediately left for the sink saying "I'll be right back!"

"All right! Let's discuss the plan!" I said.

Rohan came after a few minutes and we were discussing. After discussing, we went out for dinner at a fast food joint.

"Shit!" Priya cried out.

"What happened?" I asked.

"Aah! It's spicy! I think I ate a chilli! I need water! Now! I need-"she started but stopped when Virat grabbed a bottle and passed it to her. She, without noticing, takes it and gulps down a lot of water.

"Aa...thanks, Virat!" she says, relaxed.

"Don't mention it!" he replied, with a smirk.

"Okay...it's awkward now!" I said.

After dinner, we head back to the apartment and went to bed.

The next morning, we left for the hotel and met the staff. They were with us but they warned us that the manager shouldn't get to know about it. As the manager was a friend of our target, it was not good to tell him. Preparations were being made and I had to change the plan. I was going to test Sonam so instead of me, Sonam will target him with a sniper.

"But then we shouldn't be at the venue, right?" said Ajay.

"And also, we should go right after the job, leave at night!" said Ankita.

"Our next stop is Raipur! We can go safely from here!" said Raj.

"How about only two people go for the checking? I mean, should anything go wrong then they can check him out!" said Sanjana.

"Sonia and Rohan?" said Virat.

"No! Me and Simran!" I said.

"Okay!" she said.

"Yes! So the rest of you leave a bit later and pack up everything, fill gas! We will get the job done!" I said.

"I think the building on the right is good enough for me! It gives a good view!" said Sonam.

"Good! All yours!" I said.

"Let's do this!" said Dinesh.

It was 7:00 and we both entered the hotel. While walking inside, Simran pulls me to a side.

"What happened?" I asked.

"Why did you take me? I have my doubts on Sonam! Still!" she said.

"You're telling this now?" I asked.

"Sorry!" she said.

"It's okay, I got it covered! Roshan is keeping an eye on her!" I said.

We both left to the banquet hall of the hotel. As we got into the lift, our target was there. He was on the phone with someone and speaking in Tamil, as if we don't know. He thought we didn't know at all.

"How is she dead?" "Okay...did you put anything on search yet?" "Well, stop delaying and get off your chairs!" "At least, I've got enough protection on me!" "Well, start working, you lazy fools!"

That was a lot he said. I recorded that on my watch. After we got out, me and Simran left for the bar and sat down.

"He's stupid!" she said. "But smart!"

"Yeah, he got to know only after a day!" I said.

"Point! Oh, let's go! He's dead!" she said.

We both got up and left the hotel. Outside, Roshan calls.

"The job's done! Sonam did it!" he said.

"Good! Now let's get out of here!" I said.

We reached the apartment and got on the bike. I couldn't change so Rohan had to drive. After we got to the National Highway, we stopped at a restaurant to eat. I and Simran went in the bathroom. We finished changing in five minutes and came out. After eating, we went out.

"Let's go! You drive!" I said and tossed the keys to Rohan.

"Why?" he asked.

"I haven't slept for a while. So Priya can come and sit with you and-"I started.

"No! Sonu, I won't have a problem if you sleep on me but I won't listen to you this time!" he said.

Everybody was so surprised that I was going to let somebody else ride my bike! I never do usually!

"I will not come on the bike now! I'm sleepy!" I said.

"No, I'm not going to let you go this time!" he said.

"This time?! Rohan, I thought that I've made it clear that after all of this, I'm not going to see you again! That's it!" I said and left.

Chapter 14
Couple Targets

I got in the car and sat with Roshan, Sonam, Simran, Ajay and Virat while Priya left on the bike with Rohan.

"Why did you say that?!" asked Virat, as we both sat down at the back.

"I meant it, that's why!" I said.

"You still like him!" he said.

"No, I don't!" I replied.

"You do!" he said.

"I don't!" I said.

"Yeah, you do!" he said.

"So what?" I replied.

"So go! Tell him!" he said.

"No need!" I said.

"Why not? He likes you!" said Simran, turning back and giving a wink.

"Well, I'm not doing anything!" I said.

"Why not? You can try a pick up line!" said Sonam.

"No!" I said.

"What type of advice is that?! Would you try a pick up line?!" asked Roshan.

"I was just suggesting!" she said in a loud tone.

There was a short pause.

"Why can't you just tell him how you feel?" asked Ajay.

"Please no! It's been five years! I'm not telling him anything!" I said.

"If you won't then I surely will!" said Virat.

"I'll beat you up!" I said.

"Oh come on! Do it!" he said.

"No, later! That's final! Besides, I don't even like being near that beard of his!" I said.

"Fine! Now our next target is Vipul and Deepa Chawla!" said Simran.

"You know, we did background checks on both! Vipul is in an illegal women trafficking business which Deepa has no idea about! I got to know about it through a phone call between Vipul and Sajid Aroura!" said Ajay.

"Also, we are going to Raipur! Maybe you can meet your sister!" said Simran.

"She left for Cape town!" I said, uninterested.

"But it seems that her plane left without her!" said Ajay.

"What?" I said.

"Yeah, I got to know from the area's IG when I went there!" said Roshan.

"Hmm..." I thought.

Something was wrong. I had a bad feeling. Why didn't she get on the plane? But we reached Raipur at 11:00am. We reached an old warehouse and everybody got down. I was thinking till then. Should I go check? I, I don't know. I will have to slip out. But how...

"Come on!" said Simran.

"No, I have to go check! Aanya's in trouble! I can feel it!" I said.

"Okay, we'll leave now! I'll go tell Ajay!" she said.

"Good! And no Rohan!" I said.

"Okay!" she said and went to tell Ajay.

After a minute or two, she came out.

"I'm sorry, to get the keys from Rohan, I had to tell him!" she said.

"It's okay, let's go!" I said.

"Where are we going, actually?" she asked.

"To my grandparents' house! They died but she should be there with their servant! I know, I haven't seen her in seven years. I just talk briefly and our chats never ended properly but I just-"I started.

"It's all right! Let's go!" she said and we left.

It was 12:00pm and we reached the house. The front door was open! I knew it! Something was definitely wrong! We parked the bike and rushed in to see nobody except...a dead body. The dead body of the servant! With a bullet in his head! Shit!

"The blood looks fresh! She must have been taken last night or so!" said Simran.

Well, it was that obvious that maybe those same bad guys abducted her just like me! Damn! Why didn't she leave?! Why?! But we were interrupted by sirens of a police van. So we left immediately and were back at the warehouse by 1:10.

"Aanya's gone! Someone took her!" I said.

"I tracked her phone! She's in a bungalow! And-oh wow! It's registered in our target's names! They live there!" said Dinesh.

"And it seems that they will be home by 8:00 tomorrow!" said Sanjana.

"Good! We'll break in an hour before! But we'll have to leave after killing them, even if we can't find...yeah. That's it!" I said and left from the main hall.

I couldn't finish what I was talking about. I got scared now. If I see her dead?! I don't know what I would do! I had to save her! No choice!

In the morning, I went to check the tracker on her phone but it didn't work. Either they found it or her phone's battery is dead.

"I stayed up all night! I figured this would happen! We'll get her!" said Simran.

"I hope so!" I said.

Just then, Virat came.

"Well, what are you doing up so early?" I asked.

"Nothing, I slept a lot yesterday at noon so I just did time pass!" he said.

"What sort of time pass?" I asked.

"I was trying to call Rahul. He wasn't picking up. I talked to Priya too!" he said.

"Oh! No wonder!" said Simran.

"What were you two talking about?" I asked.

"You go ask her!" he said.

I left after a few minutes to a room in which Priya was sleeping in. I threw a pillow at her.

"Ah! What the hell?!" she groaned.

"What were you talking about with Virat? Tell me, tell me, tell me!" I asked.

"I promise, I'll tell you later! We have to get Aanya! And it seems Rahul, Virat's brother was here too! You think-"she replied.

"I know! But don't tell him!" I said.

"Yeah, he'll get hyper!" she said.

I went out. I was getting more worried. Everyone was getting ready while I was outside looking at the view of the city from the terrace. After a few minutes, a hand around my back came and I took out my hands from my forehead.

"What do you want, Rohan?" I asked.

"Nothing!" he said.

"Then why are you here?" I asked.

"I just want to say...uh..." he tarted.

"What, Rohan? I'm already annoyed enough and worried!" I said.

"We'll get her! And we'll get Rahul too!" he said.

"So he is there!" I said.

"Yeah, we got a trace on his phone! He's there with her in the basement of their house! We're ready to go! It is early but-"he started.

"It's okay, let's go!" I said.

He let go of me and we both walked downstairs. Everyone was suited up with their guns and I got suited up too.

"Ready?" I asked when we almost reached.

"Yeah!" said everybody.

"Sonu, I'm coming with you!" said Virat.

"Okay, then Rohan! Go with the rest to tear down the place!" I said.

"Got it!" he said.

Rohan looked at me and squeezed my shoulder with his hand for reassurance. I nodded and he let go. We reached and got down. We stealthily entered the compound and killed the security guards, one by one, as they approached us. I and Virat went and busted open the basement door! And we found a young boy of 16 tied up with tape! It was Rahul! Virat immediately rushed to him and took off the tape on his mouth.

"Where's Aanya?" I asked.

"They took her!" said Rahul.

"Where?!" I asked.

"They should be at home! But not for long! They are running away! That should be their car!" he said.

I heard an engine and immediately rushed outside to see a black SUV leaving! I ran after it and aimed! I shot a bullet in the tire and the car had to stop since the tire got punctured. I rushed over with Rohan, Simran and Ajay behind. There was the couple in front with a girl looking like a younger version of me. She was tied up! Simran opened the door then untied Aanya and took her away. I heard her shouting "Sonu di! I need her now!"

I rushed over to her while Ajay and Rohan kept their guns pointed at the targets.

"Sonu di, how-how did you-"she started.

I put my hand on her cheek and said "I got this! Go to Rahul with her! I got this!" then I left to the car while Simran drags Aanya away. I stepped at the left window where Deepa sat with my gun pointed.

"Both of you! Get out of the car! And don't try anything funny! Or else I shoot!" I said, sternly.

"Come on!" shouted Rohan.

Without a word, they both got out of the car and stood in the front. Immediately a few guards charged at the sight.

"Now you're dead!" said Vipul.

I signalled Ajay who in a flash, turned and shot a few bullets killing them. I pointed the tip of my gun to Vipul's fore head.

"You were going to sell my sister in your little business, weren't you? I'm sure you have no idea what I'm talking about, aren't you?" I said.

"What?" he said.

"I know you, your Sonia! Neerav and Rekha's daughter!" said Deepa.

"Good! That was my sister in the backseat! And your husband here was going to ship her away. Women trafficking, he's involved in that! Oops, she wasn't supposed to know, was she?" I said.

"Just a minute!" – She punched Vipul twice – "I'm ashamed to call you my husband!" she yelled.

"Enough!" I shouted.

"You're Rohan. You go on your father!" said Vipul, wiping the blood on his mouth.

"You don't know me! And yet you pulled the trigger! You killed them!" said Rohan.

"I'll keep this short and sweet! We've come to kill both of you and we don't care about what happens!" I said.

"You'll pay for it!" said Vipul.

I shot two bullets in him. Rohan shot a bullet in her chest. They both collapsed and fell down dead. They were finished. In a few minutes, we got in our cars and left directly from that house to the road. It was 8:00pm and we found a restaurant to eat.

Chapter 15
Reunion, in Jail

"Hey! What happened?" I asked.

"Nothing, I was just thinking that if you hadn't come in time then what would have happened! Thank you, for finding me!" she replied.

We both had eaten quickly and stood outside near the car and bikes waiting for the others.

"You're my sister, I have to find you and I will! Always!" I said.

"But we never, uh...we just never talked much so I thought I would die!" she said.

"It's okay now. You're here and so am I!" I said.

"I just can't believe it! That you're here and you're an assassin! That's cool!" she said, while sniffling.

"Hey! Come on!" I said, while giving her a hug. "I'm here now!"

"I know, I just-damn! I'm so stupid to miss my flight when I had the ticket!" she said.

"Why didn't you go?" I asked.

"Rahul was worried about his brother! So he made me stay! I had to listen because he's my...um...boyfriend!" she said.

"Isn't that nice!" I said.

I should have expected that. No wonder they both were together in the basement of the bungalow.

"Yeah, what about you?" she asked.

"I've got time!" I said, chuckling.

"I don't think so! You have quite a few targets left, don't you?" she said.

"Yeah, we do! I'm sorry but you and Rahul will be put on a plane to Cape town. It's not safe for you here!" I said.

"No! I can't leave you here! I can't go away from you again!" she said.

"You won't! I promise you, we'll make it! But you have to go because you're too young and not safe! So don't try anymore things, okay?" I said.

"Okay...I'll miss you!" she said.

"Me too!" I said.

Immediately, everyone rushed over! They all started the car and the bikes!

"CBI is all over this place! Let's go!" said Rohan.

I pushed Aanya into the car and I started my bike. Then we all suddenly revved up and left without a trace. On the bike,

"Were they here for us or a regular raid?" I asked.

"They were looking for us, Sonu!" he said.

"Okay!" I said.

"What if they catch us at the airport?" he asked.

"We'll try our best to avoid them!" I said.

"By the way, Virat and Priya are back together!" said Rohan.

"How the hell?" I asked.

"The day before yesterday, I heard them! Priya first refused but then he said to give another shot at them! So she said okay!" he said.

"Wow! Just like school!" I said.

"Better than school!" he said.

We changed highways then stopped at a hotel and stayed there for the night.

In the morning, we left at 7:00 on AH 46 to Sambhalpur to drop Aanya and Rahul at the airport. We reached there by 12:30 and I dropped them at the gate. Virat bid good bye to Rahul at the entrance of the airport. After they checked in, Rohan came. While walking out of the airport,

"Why did you come?" I asked.

"It's getting late, the Police is here!" he said.

"Here, in the sense?" I asked.

We reached outside and they were waiting for us a little hidden in the airport parking. But while we were on our way, suddenly a few men in grey came and surrounded us! Those same people in black and white suited men to kill me!

"I hope you remember me! We remember you, Sonia! And I would love to show our boss who we got! It's been a while, I was literally chasing you! And yet, you both and we are here finally! Come on! You are under arrest for the murder of Sajid Aroura, Deepa and Vipul Chawla and Avanti Singh!" said the leader in front of me, pointing his gun at me.

Two other guys came and handcuffed us. They started to drag us away! I tried to search for the rest but no! They were gone! They ran away! The guys pushed me and Rohan in one car and we rode away! In the car, Rohan struggled but then they held him down!

"Don't struggle or we're dead!" I said.

"Yes, do listen to her!" said one guy.

We reached an old building. An old prison. In one of the prison cells, they un-cuffed me and threw me in while shutting the door. In the prison cell opposite to me, they did the same with Rohan. I struggled to open the bars but no use. Rohan tried as well. I knew that we couldn't do it so I sat down on the dusty ground.

"Enough, Rohan! It's no use trying!" I said.

He stopped and sat down in his cell.

"How did they find us?!" he asked.

"Sonam! I'm sure!" I said.

"Why is she doing this?!" he asked.

"Two reasons: One can be that she is selfish and she joined them and another can be that this was really unexpected." I said.

"First reason sounds realistic!" he said.

"Yeah! After we get out, I'll have a chat with her!" I said.

"How do we get out?" he said.

"We wait. They will come!" I said.

"And if they don't?" he asked.

"Trust me, they are family! They will come!" I said.

"I trust you!" he said.

We waited for maybe, well, let's calculate. 12:30pm we were at the airport and at 1:00 we were taken away. I felt hungry and didn't have anything for quite some time. Maybe it's 3:00. We have been in this jail cell for two hours. The men in black and white came and opened the gates. They hand cuffed us again and dragged us outside the building. As they were going to push us in the car, I suddenly notice a few people on top of the adjoining buildings and smirked for it was our team. They are here! Just after seeing them, they started shooting accurately and all the ten guys in suits were dead.

I kneeled down and checked one guy's pockets for keys, found them then opened Rohan's handcuffs and he then opened mine. Everyone came down and first, I was hugged by Priya. Then Virat and Roshan came and hugged me. Simran then hugged me. I noticed that there were a few more people.

"Sonia and Rohan! Meet my friends working under Arjit Aroura! They are ready to assist us!" said Dinesh.

"Good! Let's go somewhere else first! Get the cars!" I said and everybody left. "Sonam, come here!"

Everybody left and she came.

"Who gave the tip? Or was it just a mere coincidence that they happened to show up?" I asked.

"I didn't give a tip! I swear!" she said.

"Well, I can't believe you now! But just remember, I'm watching you!" I said.

We all left to an old house nearby the airport. Arjit was the main reason of our parent's torture. He sent threats of their killing.

"So who's in charge?" asked the boss.

"That would be me!" I said.

"Okay!" he said.

We discussed the plan while studying the layout of his home. It was a huge bungalow as well and it was very big with many rooms. He lived alone but with a lot of money his parents always sent him. Before the separation of his parents, they were good but the reason of our parents' murders, Sarita Aroura filed for divorce. Arjit supported his father but Sarita walked out on him and sajid. She works at a Charity and runs an NGO at the same time. Sometimes she does a few arms deals like storing them safely without suspicions. Arjit is a CID detective.

It was 4:00pm and we reached a few houses away. We parked and started walking towards his house. While walking, I noticed Virat and Priya at a distance. Simran was walking with me and I spotted Rohan in the front with Ajay.

"Come on!" she said.

"What?" I asked.

"I saw your face when you were taken out of the jail. You both were bonding!" she said.

"What are you trying to say?" I asked.

"Try something! Maybe not a pick up line! But something close to that!" she said.

"I do want to pull something off but Ajay is there!" I said.

"I got this!" she said.

We both sped up to the front of the group. Ajay was immediately pulled back by Simran and I popped right next to Rohan.

"Rohan!" I said, while loading my gun.

"Yeah, tell!" he said.

"For this target, you'll have to stay with me! Close to me! Okay or not?" I asked.

"Yeah, okay!" he said.

"And by the way!" I said.

"What?" he asked.

"Thank you for helping me to find Aanya!" I said.

"I didn't do anything!" he said.

"Seriously, you don't know how much you did!" I said.

"I just told you that we'll get her!" he said.

"So that motivated me! I mean us!" I said.

"Really?" he asked.

"Yes..." I said.

"Hmm..." he murmered.

We reached. We took out our guns except me and Rohan. We were taken inside the front door. The first part of the plan was to pretend to be prisoners and till then, the rest of them will go and take out the guards and the cameras of the house.

Chapter 16
The son

The doors opened and we both were forcibly taken inside. The boss grabs my arm and another guy grabs Rohan's arm. After a flight of stairs, we were walking in the hall. The house was very fancy and trendy. Definitely he had a lot of money. We reached the end of the hall and in front of two doors. The officers with us opened the doors and dragged us in. it was his home office. On the desk was our target's feet and he was sitting on his chair. He got up and stood with his arms crossed.

Oh my! He was so hot! Damn! He's well built! His hair curled up, he's fair, wearing a black t shirt and jeans with sandals. Damn, he is so hot! It's going to be quite hard to shoot him!

"Rohan?" I whispered.

"Yeah?" he asked softly.

"You will have to kill him!" I said.

"I can't! Why can't you?" he asked.

"Did you see him?" I asked.

"What? He's not that tough for you!" he said.

How can I say this to him?!

"I can't concentrate!" I said.

"Oh! Okay I will try! But you also!" he said.

"Fine!" I said.

He nodded.

Our hot target started to speak.

"Well! Sonia and Rohan! I was waiting for you both! I know all about you both and your parents' deaths! Each one and everyone!" he said, while he was roaming around us.

He was about to touch me when,

"Don't touch me!" I shouted.

"Don't touch her!" Rohan shouted.

We both shouted together. Then we paused to look at each other for a moment.

"I will really enjoy finishing you both just like your cousin, you remember her? Shona?" he asked.

I was shocked. How did he know her?! He killed her?! Really?

"Yes, I killed Shona! She was venturing in our scheme a little too far. So I finished her! After that, my mother did leave me!" he continued.

"You killed Shona?! You killed her?!" I yelled out in anger.

"Oh yes, I did! And I will get away with it for sure!" he said.

I struggled from the boss' hands but then he whispered "No! Not now!" and I stopped.

"They are under me!" said Arjit.

"Whatever!" said Rohan.

"Oh, are you undermining me?" he asked.

"Maybe I am!" said Rohan.

"Rohan, keep stalling!" I whispered.

He slightly nodded at me and continued.

"Well, you are wrong!" said Arjit.

"Oh really?" said Rohan.

"You don't know me and you don't know what I'm capable of!" he said.

"Same here!" replied Rohan.

Immediately, our team barged in the room and surrounded him. The boss let me go and Rohan was also let go. I took my gun from Priya and Rohan took his from Roshan. We pointed our guns at him. In a flash, we put a bullet each, through his chest, before Arjit could take out his gun and he collapsed on the ground.

We left his house after giving the share of money to the officers. Then we had decided to stay at the old house for the night then leave in the morning for Kolkata. Yes, our next target Sarita Aroura, was there. It was 7:00 and I was on the terrace. Priya came.

"Hey!" she said.

"Hi, what's up with you and Virat?" I asked.

"Nothing! Well, a lot! I was wrong! He really did change! For me!" she said.

"I told you! Everybody thinks so too!" I said.

Rohan then appeared.

"Uh, Priya! I need to talk to Sonia! Alone!" he said.

"Yeah! Sure! See you!" she said and left.

"Hey! What's up?" I asked.

"So what's wrong with you?" he asked.

"I'm totally fine!" I said. "Oh, and I'm sorry for that thing I said about not having to do anything with you after all of this!"

"See? That's exactly what is wrong with you!" he said.

"What's wrong with what I said?" I asked.

"You're getting soft! Do tell me why!" he said.

"No, I'm not!" I said.

"Yes, you are!" he said.

"No, I'm not! Stop asking stupid questions!" I said and left.

It was 7:30 and we both were called for dinner. We went downstairs to see everyone round together at a huge table and we all sat down. As we were eating,

"So, I've loaded all the bikes and the car with a full tank so we'll leave for Kolkata tomorrow!" said Dinesh.

"Sonia, did you call your uncle?" asked Sanjana.

"Yeah, he's ready to take the bike!" I said.

The plan was to go to Kolkata, finish our job there and sell our vehicle and give away our bikes to our relatives. Then take a flight to Delhi to finish off our last target and leave for Cape town.

"That's good!" said Ankita.

"But there is a problem!" said Raj.

"What?" we asked.

"The police are too strict there! And they can't help us!" said Raj.

"Then how can we make our job easier?" asked Roshan.

"What if we directly go to her workplace and kill her? It's in a slum area so less police!" said Rohan.

"Good idea, Rohan! When did you get so smart?" asked Ajay.

"It's not smart! It's common sense!" he said, while giving a glance at me.

Damn! Common sense? What is he pulling at?

"We'll make a full-proof plan when we reach there. No helpers, only us!" I said.

"Yeah, you're right! But if we don't have help, how can we even get there properly?" asked Virat.

"We'll see about that later!" I said.

We finished our dinner and went to bed. I was sleeping next to Priya when she suddenly wakes me up. I sit along with her.

"What happened?" I asked.

"I received word from your uncle before I gave the phone to you!" she said.

"What?" I asked.

"Your grandmother is dying. She has a day to live." Said Priya.

"Oh, well, anything else?" I asked.

"Sonu, as soon as we get there, you have to go visit her. She has some aspects of her will to discuss with you! Okay?" said Priya.

"Sure. And Priya?" I asked.

"Yes?" she asked.

"You're the best!" I said.

"You're welcome!" she said.

We both went back to bed.

In the morning, we left at 5:00am and reached the highway in another half an hour. We were on the AH 49. At 7:00, we stopped for breakfast. I was sitting opposite to Rohan and eating.

"Uh, Rohan?" I called out.

"Hm?" he replied, while eating.

"I have some other work when we get to Kolkata. I need you to come along!" I said.

"So are you ordering or requesting?" he asked.

"You decide!" I said.

"Hm...I'll take requesting! It's nicer that way! Okay, I'll come with you!" he said.

"Thanks..." I said.

"But what type of other work is at Kolkata?" he asked.

"You'll get to know later!" I said, disinterested to tell him.

We all continued to eat. After a few minutes, we left. We again stopped to have lunch at about 12:30. We sat down at a table.

"Okay...Sonia! What do you want to order?" he asked.

"Not me...I'll just have soup!" I said.

"Really?" he asked.

"Yeah, I swear! I'm fine!" I said.

He nodded and moved ahead. I didn't feel like eating much. I was only thinking about her. How she might be. It's been some time since I've seen her and my uncle.

Later on, after lunch, we were back on the road. We reached Kolkata at 2:30pm. We got another warehouse to stay at. When we got down and kept our bags, Rohan and I left. Priya covered for us. After an hour, we reached a small street. At the end, there was a house, quite big. We went inside, and while going upstairs,

"Can you tell me now?" he asked.

"My grandmother is going to die today so I have to get what's left for me." I said.

"Oh, sorry!" he said.

We reached her room. At the entrance, my uncle was there and he hugged me.

"You're on time. She was just asking for you!" he said.

"Okay..." I said. "Come on!"

We both went inside. There on the bed, she was lying down. I kneeled down next to her and caught her hand. The chat was in Bangla.

"Hi! How are you?" I asked, with difficulty.

"Come closer, beta! I can't hear you!" she said, with great difficulty too.

She beckoned and I sat down next to her. She gave me a paper and a box.

"Keep it! It will help you!" she said.

"Thank you!" I said.

"You've grown and so have I! It's good to see you!" she said.

"You too!" I said.

She slowly closed her eyes and stopped her breath.

CHAPTER 17
THE DIVORCEE

After her cremation ceremony, I, Rohan and my uncle chat. It was 4:00pm.

"So, this is Rohan! We both used to go to school together!" I said.

"Oh, nice to meet you!" uncle said.

"Same here!" said Rohan.

"Well, I guess this is the last time-"uncle started.

"Please don't say that! We'll meet again!" I said.

"Surely!" piped in Rohan.

"Well, that's good to hear!" he said.

"Well, we'll have to go!" I said.

"It's okay! Don't open anything of that box until you leave India!" uncle said.

"Okay!" I said.

We bid good bye. We left and were back at the warehouse by 5:00. When we got inside, everybody was waiting for us to discuss the plan.

"Where were you guys at?" asked Roshan.

"Long story!" we both said.

We got to planning. We weren't going to break in, we were going to enter disguised as a mafia goon with an entire army of goons right into her office.

In the morning, we all got up a bit late, or maybe that was just me. Nobody woke me up. Maybe because I slept very late as I was thinking over what had happened today. It was 8:00am so I got up and went outside to see nobody except Rohan...wait!

He looked different! He shaved off his beard! Damn! Awesome! Finally, he did it!

"Hey, where is everybody?!" I called out and asked.

"Beats me! Get ready and come! We'll find them!" he said with a smirk.

"Two minutes!" I said.

I quickly got ready by freshening up, putting on a jacket only since I didn't change from my jeans. Wait! Where is my gun and bag?! I went down the stairs and Rohan was waiting for me.

"When did you get up?" I asked.

"7:30!" he said.

"Okay..." I said.

We both stopped talking for a while. I was not able to take off my eyes from him. Damn! He looked really good!

"So should we go look for them or wait here?" I asked.

"Let's go. After you!" he said.

"Thanks..." I said.

We went out and shut the door of the old warehouse then left towards the nearby streets on foot. While walking, we saw a few black jeeps on the road. I pulled Rohan to a side inside a house's compound wall.

"What happened?" he asked.

"Sorry" – I took my hand off him – "but I think I know why everybody left!" I said.

"I didn't understand!" he said.

"Did you take your gun?" I asked.

"Yeah, all of them!" he said.

"Good! Those black jeeps are from the CBI! I think they are getting doubts about us!" I said.

"Oh!" he said.

At that time, Virat called me.

"Yeah, what's up? Where are you?" I asked.

"Who's that?" whispered Rohan.

"Virat!" I replied.

"We're two streets right from you! You both come! I and Priya will be standing there!" he said.

"Got it!" I said and cut the call.

"Let's go! They are two streets from here!" I said.

"Okay...hmm..." he muttered.

"What?" I asked.

"Nothing!" he said. "Let's go!"

"No, what's wrong?" I asked while we started to walk.

"Him!" he said as we saw Virat.

"Don't tell me that you're still jealous!" I said.

"I've always been jealous! What do you care?" he said.

"I care! You're jealous because you like me, right?" I said.

"No!" he said.

"Then what?" I asked.

"It's because I love you!" he said.

There was a pause and we stopped walking.

"What?" I asked.

"I love you! That's it! Done!" he said.

"Not done! Rohan please, you can't say that now!" I said.

"Why not?" he asked.

"This isn't the time! We still have to finish our job and reach Cape town! I don't want it now!" I said.

"I just said it! I don't expect anything to happen! Just that you could say it too or..." he said, while coming a bit closer to me.

"Dude!" – I pushed him back – "Distance! Right now!" I said.

"What's wrong? You were hitting on me before! Now today that changed!" he said.

"It's just that- I mean- Arh! It's complicated!" I said.

"Now you're confusing me!" h said.

"Good! Stay like that!" I said.

"Seriously, enough! What's your problem?!" he asked. "You want this, right?"

"Yeah but-"I started.

"Well, I want this too!" he said.

"Yes, but not now! It won't work out now!" I said.

"Why can't it?" he asked.

"It's a lot of pressure! First, we should finish this!" I said. "Let's go! They're waiting and don't do or say anything stupid!"

"Like what, babe?" he asked.

"Like that!" I said, annoyed and I went ahead.

Virat and Priya came and we all went inside a house. In a room, I checked that my bag and Rohan's bag was there. Good.

"We're ready! You get ready, Sonu! We'll load our things in the car!" said Priya.

"Cool! Let's go, Rohan!" I said.

He comes into a room with me and we get ready, one at a time. When he came out, finally, I grabbed my gun and loaded it.

"How long do you take?" I asked, while loading my gun.

"Well, I can't be as fast as you, right?" he said.

We both went and sat in the car while Virat and Priya get on my bike. We left at 10:00. We went on the road which was straightaway going into an area downtown in Kolkata. It had old buildings and we stopped n front of one which looked smashed up. It still had three floors. We got down. First, it was me then Rohan who got down, then after us everybody else got down and followed. We reached the entrance and there was an office receptionist.

"May I help you, sir?" she asked.

"Shoot her!" I said.

Immediately Virat came forward and pointed his gun at her.

"But why?!" she cried out.

"She's the boss! All questions will be asked to her!" said Rohan.

"Is Sarita Aroura here?" I asked, through my gritted teeth.

"You mean Sarita Bhattacharya? Third floor!" she said in fright.

"Good!" I said.

We climbed up the stairs and went in front of a room door. I busted it open. We all went inside and I saw her on her chair. I pointed my gun at her face.

"Who are you?!" she asked, taken aback.

"Take a wild guess!" I said.

"Rekha sure doesn't look like that! Who are you?!" she asked.

"Her daughter!" I said.

"What's your name?" she asked.

"Quit stalling!" I said.

Suddenly, Rohan grabbed her gun which suddenly came out and threw it back which Simran caught then passed it to Ajay.

"Anything else you'd like to try?" asked Rohan.

"No..." she said. "I've gotten old! And I know what I've done! So do it!"

I shot two bullets in her chest. She collapsed on her chair. I slowly lowered my gun and left. Everybody else came a few minutes later after taking care of the body. Rohan came before.

"Hey!" he said.

"What do you want?" I asked.

"Uh...nothing, just-"he started but everybody else had come down already.

I gave a sign saying later and he saw it. We all left then gave our car and bikes away. By the airport bus, we reached with our stuff in time and checked in. we boarded our flight and when I reached my seat and sat down, Rohan came and sat down next to me after storing his bag up. He was somewhat glad.

"What's up, babe?" he said.

Next to me, there was Priya, who heard that and giggled. Damn!

"You tell me, Rohan!" I said and looked at him, sceptically.

"Oho!" said Priya.

"Shut up, please!" I whispered to her.

"You'd better-"I started by pointing a finger at him.

"I'd better what?" he asked, grabbing my hand softly.

"You're impossible!" I said.

"And so are you! But what we can be, it's possible!" he said.

"But it's not possible now!" I said.

"Oh come on! Priya and Virat are together!" he said.

"That's because they were with each other before too!" I said.

"Then what about later? After all of this?" he asked.

"I'll consider!" I said.

"You're impossible!" he said.

"So are you!" I said.

Priya still giggled. Damn! This went on for the entire flight! Shit!

Chapter 18
The Final target!

We reached Delhi with delays but at 8:00pm. We were getting off the plane but Rohan wasn't waking up. He was sleeping on my shoulder. I dozed off as well then he did.

"Rohan...get up! Come on!" I said.

"Huh?" he asked, groggily.

"Get up! Both of you! We have to go!" said Raj.

"Huh! Ow! My head!" he said, while we stood.

"I didn't hit you this time!" I said.

We got up the got down and left the plane through the passages. We left the airport at 8:30 and took the airport liner to a far point. When we got down, we walked into a street. Then we stop at an old, normal looking house. A guy and a girl stood at the entrance. They were Sourabh and Soumya. They were friends of Dinesh.

"Come quick!" said Soumya.

"For the night, it's all sorted. Then leave in the morning. Okay?" said Sourabh.

"Sure! Thanks!" said Dinesh.

We all went in then changed and flopped down to sleep. As I was about to, I see Rohan out on the balcony. He was sitting on a bed with his back on the wall. I went outside and sat down next to him.

"Hi..." he said.

"Hey..." I said as I scooted back and sat next to him.

"Not sleepy?" he asked.

"I should ask you that!" I said.

"I'll sleep out here!" he said.

"You won't be able to sleep out here!" I said.

"Well, I'll manage! You go inside and sleep!" he said.

He took out a fat blanket and covered himself.

"No, I'll stay!" I said.

We both shared the blanket.

"It's really starry tonight!" he said.

"Yeah, it is!" I said.

"Thanks, Sonu!" he said.

"For what? You didn't want to be here!" I said.

"Now I do! You found me! And taught me a lot!" he said.

"It's okay..." I said.

"So tomorrow..." he said.

"The last one...if we survive this...I hope we do!" I said.

"If we escaped this much then who said that we can't do that?" he asked.

I got up and went inside.

"Hey! What did I say?" he asked.

I came back with my tablet and got in the covers next to him.

"Oh, you went to get that!" he said.

I surfed through a few files I had downloaded before. I showed him a document of transactions made by Prakash.

"The first few are from his bank account to his team of hackers. The last targets of the hit list. They all will be at the hotel we are going to! We definitely need more people to kill them. So Dinesh arranged for the police to arrive. Higher intelligence officers also got to know so we should escape before they arrive. So we have to kill them before they get here! It will be complicated so keep up!" I said.

"Damn this will be hard!" he said.

"Yes, it will! So you ready for tomorrow?" I asked.

"I don't have a choice, do I?" he said.

"You don't!" I said.

We continued to talk for some more time then we both slept there.

In the morning, we were woken up by Priya.

"Huh?" I woke up.

"What's the time?" asked Rohan.

He was again on my shoulder.

"It's 8:30! Were you both out here all night?" she asked, while giggling.

"It looks like it!" said Rohan.

"You mind getting off of me now?" I asked.

"Sure, babe! See you!" he got up and left.

"What's going on?" she asked.

"He said 'I love you', I said that I don't want this now! He was like why and I said later. So now he's hitting on me!" I said.

"Good!" she said.

She left inside and when I looked back she was jumping up in joy shouting out "Yes! Yes! Yes! Finally!" and going. We all got ready and bid Sourabh and Soumya good bye then we left. We took a bus to the airport. But the airport bus liner stopped at a bus stop before the airport and we got down in front of a hotel. It was 9:40 and we went inside.

"Are you sure about this, dude?" the manager asked.

"Yeah, man!" he said.

Our last targets were Tanya Sharma, Pradeep Desai, John Ryan, Amy Ross and Prashant Oberoi. All of those people are his personal hackers. They can find out anything and everything about any person. Even if that person is nowhere in the internet, they can still find that person. Prashant is one of the largest business tycoons in the world. He's only 52. But I definitely won't leave the chance. Our parents' hits were first ordered by this guy. All because of him, our lives are ruined! All ruined!

It was 8:30pm again, till then we were seeing all the rooms. I observed everyone coming and starting to enjoy themselves. I was filled with anger. Rohan came and stood next to me.

"What do you want?" I asked.

"The targets know who we are, they know that we both are here but not about the others here with us!" he replied.

"That's good but bad too!" I said. "Anything else?"

"The police will take half an hour to get here so that's our window of time. We should go now!" he said.

"Okay...come on!" I said.

I was going to leave but he doesn't follow me.

"Hey!" I said. "What happened?"

"I...I can't...I can't do it! I'm too scared!" he said, while sniffling.

"Come on!" I said, coming back and going close to him. "Look at me!"

He didn't. I pulled his face towards mine.

"I'm there, right?" I said.

"You aren't enough, are you?" he said.

I pulled him into a hug. A very tight one.

"I'm enough for you! We'll survive this!" I said.

"I hope so!" he said, muffled.

We pulled away. We then left into a room after again checking outside whether everyone was there or not. Just as we came inside, two guys in black and white suits closed the doors and stood in front of them. In front of us was Prashant on a chair. Amy and Tanya were on his left and Pradeep and john were on his right.

"Sonia! Rohan! Good to see you! It's been a few years, hasn't it?" said Prashant.

Meanwhile, our team was taking out all the security of the men in black and white and they were going to come. Till then we just had to make conversation with him.

"Ten years, right?" I said.

"Yes! You got it! Anyway, I didn't know that you two were capable of killing all of my friends, colleagues and what not!" he said.

"A lot of people under estimate that!" said Rohan.

I noticed an air vent slowly opening on the left and a rope was let down around Amy's neck. Suddenly it pulls up and Amy was choked to death without a sound.

"Well, let me tell you why I ordered that hit on your parents!" he said.

At that time, in the same way, on the right, John was choked. Then Tanya and Pradeep were choked. Slowly, everyone came in through the vents.

"Let's just cut to the chase, actually! We are going to kill you two!" he said.

"I'd like to see you try!" I said.

Me and Rohan Immediately took out our guns and pointed at Prashant. Our team behind did the same.

"You know how this will end! So lower your gun!" said Prashant.

He thought that his hackers were still there, hah! Not!

"I won't do it!" I said.

He turned around to give an order but was shocked to see none of them alive. Three...two...one! It was lightening fast when suddenly more of our team barged in the doors as well. I stepped forward and shot a bullet in his stomach.

"You've ruined my entire life!! Just by finishing off my parents!! I hope you're happy now because you can go to hell! Just where you came from!" I screamed out on his almost dead face.

Rohan came forward and shot another bullet in his chest and Prakash collapsed.

"I was always pitied! I never had a fun time! I was always alone! Nobody would understand me! And that's all because of you!!" he yelled.

I kicked him twice then we all left leaving him there. It was almost 10:00 when we reached the airport. We checked in our gate and boarded our flight. Again Rohan sat down next to me. I was next to the window with Rohan in the middle and another one of us, Sanjana.

I don't know why, but as soon as the plane took off, I felt like sleeping right then. But I chose not to. Rohan noticed and pulled my head on his shoulder and I slept. He slept as well.

I woke up at 7:00...and was still in the plane. Sanjana also was awake and she informed that the plane will reach Cape Town at 10:30. Rohan was still sleeping. When he woke up, it was 9:30.

"Good morning!" he said.

"Morning..." I replied.

"We did it...yes!" he started.

I was brooding. I was still thinking that something could still happen. But what? And will it be me?

"Come on, Sonu! Don't worry!" he said.

"I have to, Rohan! It's not easy to get away with this and go live in a place for the rest of our lives!" I said, softly.

Rohan said no more. Sanjana nodded saying "I can say that you aren't wrong!" I was getting more worried. I got up and left for the bathroom. Sanjana came too and in front of the bathroom, we talked.

"You'd better start talking!" I said.

"You and Rohan are supposed to get arrested when we get down. But it won't happen!" she said.

"Then who's going?" I asked.

"Yeah, who's going?" asked Rohan.

He came and was standing behind. I turned back and saw him.

"Sonam and Roshan!" said Sanjana.

"Are you-"Rohan was going too loud and I closed his mouth.

"Are you crazy?!" I whispered.

"I don't have any other choice!" she said.

"But for what?" I asked.

"Possession of arms!" she replied. "Unlicensed ones!"

"So in South Africa law, how long is the jail term?" Rohan asked.

"Two years." She said.

We couldn't say anymore. We went back to our seats. But I went and sat down next to Sonam while Rohan sat down next to Roshan.

"Yes, Sonia?" she asked, while sniffling a bit.

"I'm sorry!" I said.

"For what?" she asked.

"Everything...high school, Rohan, accusing you...but why did you put that drug packet?" I asked.

"Instead of seeing you killed, I wanted you in jail! I never liked you so much but I do care! Now I'll be gone for two years. I hope you're happy now that Rohan's all yours! I don't like him!" she said.

"I'll keep visiting you! Even I never liked you so much but do you remember what you said at school?" I asked.

"Yeah, I said that I would consider you...better than my family, who I left!" she said, with a tear rolling down.

She left her family as they were only interested in getting her married. That's why she left home and she robbed for money, of course.

I hugged her tightly.

"Come on! Just two years!" I said.

"This is my entire fault! And that stupid Roshan just has to take the blame on him too!" she said.

"Can't you see that he loves you?!" I said.

"I can't see that, okay?" she said.

"But she's right! I do!" said Roshan when he came.

I got up and went back to my seat. Later on, a while later, we got down the plane and entered the airport. At the gate entrance, as soon as we came out, the police arrived and handcuffed Sonam and Roshan by saying the usual statement and were about to leave when I stop them.

"Officer, a minute!" I said.

He stepped back a little.

"You'll come out soon! Okay?" I said.

"I know!" she said.

They left when I pulled away. We came out of the airport and everybody's families were waiting there. So was Avinash.

I ran and first hugged Arun.

"I thought you were gone!" he said.

"No, I'm here! I'm right here!" I said.

Naina gave me a big hug too. Aanya was there too and I gave her a hug. Sameer interrupted and gave a big hug.

"I thought I lost you! I'm sorry! I'm so sorry!" he said.

"It's okay! It's okay..." I said.

Everybody was rejoicing with their family. It was finally done!

Epilogue

Two years later...

I reach the Ladies' Prison Facility situated on the outskirts of Cape Town. Nearby it was a Men's Prison Facility too. I reach the gate to see Rohan going in. I avoided him and I wait at an office for a while. After a few minutes, Sonam was brought out in handcuffs and one officer opened them for me. She immediately hugged me and we both started to walk out.

"So now I'm out!" she said. "I've missed you!"

"I've missed you too!" I said.

"So where do I stay?" she asked.

"I don't know but for now you can stay with me then see later!" I said.

"Thanks!" she said.

We stopped. In front of us were Rohan and Roshan. They stopped too. After a moment, they both gave a big, tight hug to each other. After a few minutes, I and Sonam left for our house. Sonam took out her things. I left her with Naina and I went to a restaurant down the road. It had "Sanjana's" written on the top. I came inside and high fived Priya. I went into the kitchen and knuckle punched Dinesh and Avinash too then I started my shift. It was 4:00pm.

"How's Sonam and Roshan?" asked Simran.

"They're good! But I didn't stay there for long!" I said.

"What's the problem with Rohan?! You both didn't talk for one and a half year! Why?" she asked.

"I don't know, Simran! Okay, I don't! It's like high school all over again!" I said.

My shift ended at 7:00. That's when Rohan came for his shift. I went upstairs to the terrace with the box that my grandmother gave me. I set it down and opened it. It had a bundle of notes in it and a picture of my parents. I shed a tear or two when I looked at it. I started to cry more and I kept the box aside then kept crying more! I finally cried! I finally let it all out! As much as I held, I let it all go now. At that time, someone came up and stood right next to me.

"Sonu, please stop crying!" Rohan said, giving me a hug.

I couldn't. I had to let it all go out. After a few minutes, I stopped. But tears kept coming out.

"Sorry...I couldn't hold my tears anymore!" I said.

"It's really okay. Anyway, I wanted to talk to you!" he said.

I wiped my face.

"Tell, what happened?" I asked.

"You're not talking to me these days!" he said.

"We don't get to meet. Our shifts are different! We don't get time on the weekends and you don't talk to me!" I said.

"I'm talking now, aren't I?" he said.

"Very funny..." I said.

"Now would you be my girlfriend?" he asked. "The job was done; we are safe in our home now!"

"Are you sure about that?" I asked. "I mean the farewell..."

"Leave that! We are not in school anymore! Now smile and do what you want! I will also do it!" he said.

I gave a small smile.

"Okay..." I said, looking at him.

"Wait! What are you going to do?" he asked.

"This!" I said.

I leaned onto him and kissed him with both of my hands on his face. He kissed me back with one hand on my back to pull me closer and one on my cheek. As we pulled away,

"I did what I want, are you happy now?!" I asked.

"So you are my girlfriend now!" he said.

"Yes, I am!" I said.

He kissed me again at that and I kissed him back. We went a while later to finish our shift and finally, it was all over and no worry was left.